STAR WARS

THE EMPIRE STRIKES BACK

SO YOU WANT TO BE A JEDI?

AN ORIGINAL RETELLING OF *STAR WARS: THE EMPIRE STRIKES BACK*

BY *NEW YORK TIMES* BEST-SELLING AUTHOR

ADAM GIDWITZ

DISNEP

LUCASFILM
PRESS

Los Angeles • New York

Printed in the United States of America

First Edition, September 2015

1 3 5 7 9 10 8 6 4 2

FAC-008598-15219

ISBN 978-1-4847-0914-6

Library of Congress Control Number on file

Reinforced binding

Interior art by Ralph McQuarrie and Joe Johnston

Cover art by Khoa Ho

Design by Pamela Palacio and Jason Wojtowicz

Visit the official *Star Wars* website at: www.starwars.com.

SUSTAINABLE FORESTRY INITIATIVE

Certified Sourcing

www.sfiprogram.org

SFI-00993

This Label Applies to Text Stock Only

To all my Ben Kenobis and all my Yodas

AUTHOR'S NOTE

ARE YOU SURPRISED that I've written this book?

I may seem a strange choice to retell *The Empire Strikes Back*. I am known, where I am known at all, for fairy tales. Particularly the dark, scary kind.

I started working on fairy tales in 2008. I was a substitute librarian at a school in Brooklyn, and I picked up a book of Grimm's tales to read to a class of second graders. They were entertained, enthralled, enriched, and, to be honest, slightly traumatized. Inspired by this experience, I wrote my first novel, *A Tale Dark and Grimm*, which tells the "true" story of Hansel and Gretel by retelling many of the scarier, weirder, lesser-known Grimm tales.

My next two books, *In a Glass Grimmly* and *The Grimm Conclusion*, follow a similar model.

What do I know, then, about *The Empire Strikes Back*?

More than I thought, it turns out.

You may be aware that George Lucas always thought of *Star Wars* as a fairy tale. He said as much at a banquet honoring the great scholar of mythology Joseph Campbell: "I set out to write a children's film. I had an idea of doing a modern fairy tale." Later, in an interview with Bill Moyers for the PBS series *The Power of Myth*, Lucas said about *Star Wars*, "If it's a tool that can be used to make old stories be new, and relate to younger people, that's what the whole point was."

Well, that's what *I* was trying to do with Grimm's fairy tales. To make the old stories new. To help younger people see the brilliance, the terror, the hilarity, and the beauty of those classic tales. Lucas also said that he was "telling an old myth in a new way," that he was "localizing it for the end of the millennium." And now I have the extreme privilege of taking what I wholeheartedly believe is the greatest modern fairy tale and retelling it in book form—and in so doing, localizing it for the young people of our new millennium.

People sometimes complain that Luke Skywalker is not much of a character. He does not brim with personality, as Han Solo and Princess Leia do. He is a little bland. A little empty.

Which is just as it should be. The hero of a fairy tale must be empty. What do we know of Cinderella, except that she has to work in the ashes and her family is mean to her? Do we know her sense of humor? Her taste in literature? Her opinions on the politics of her kingdom? Of course not. That would ruin the story. Because the point of Cinderella is that we can put ourselves in her shoes (which, according to the Brothers Grimm, were made of gold, not glass). We all feel like Cinderella sometimes—mistreated, unappreciated, with great potential that has yet to be recognized. Her story has endured for so long, and in so many different cultures, exactly for that reason. Because she is so universal. So universally empty.

Many modern heroes are products of that mold. Huckleberry Finn isn't—you'd know him if you met him, even if he didn't tell you his name. But Harry Potter is. He doesn't have a sharply drawn personality, the way Ron and Hermione do. What do we know about Harry? That he's brave? That he cares for his friends? Frodo Baggins is another example. We know Samwise well. Even Bilbo is an idiosyncratic little hero, bobbing from breakfast to elevenses with a grumpy, frumpy, goodwilled reluctance. Frodo has some of that, but not much. Mostly, he's brave and good.

These heroes are not full characters. They are empty. Intentionally so. They are avatars for the reader. They are empty so we can inhabit them, so we can do their deeds, live their lives, and learn their lessons. Luke is such a character. Empty as a pair of shoes.

In his *Power of Myth* series, Bill Moyers said to

George Lucas, "I hear so many young people today talk about a world that is emptied of heroism—that there are no more heroic things to do." Lucas responded, "Everybody has a choice of being a hero or not being a hero, every day of their lives."

I wrote this book to give *you* that choice. I've measured those shoes just for you.

Will you put them on?

ADAM GIDWITZ

INTRODUCTION

S O YOU WANT to be a Jedi? I get that. It seems cool. You can move things with your mind. Control people with your thoughts. Oh, and the lightsabers. Yeah, those are awesome. But listen, it's not all mind control and weaponized flashlights.

Being a Jedi requires patience and strength and self-awareness. And training. Lots of training.

You still want to be a Jedi?

Tell you what. I'm going to tell you a story. Not just *a* story. *The* story. The story of one of the greatest Jedi ever. As I tell it, I'm going to give you some tests. To see if you've got what it takes.

If you're afraid, I don't blame you. Most folks

don't have what it takes. Most folks are just ordinary. Which is okay. There is nothing wrong with ordinary. But if you're ordinary, you can't be a Jedi.

Do you want to hear the story? And do you want to undergo the tests?

Do you still want to be a Jedi?

Okay.

This is the story of a young man. His name was Luke Skywalker.

Now, even though this story is about him, I'm not going to tell it that way.

You want to become a Jedi.

He became one of the greatest Jedi of all.

If you want to follow in his footsteps, you need to walk in his shoes.

I mean, *really* walk in his shoes. And wear his clothes. And carry his lightsaber. And share his friends. And fight his enemies. You need, for the duration of this story, to become Luke.

If you do, you will have walked the long, difficult, dangerous path of a Jedi.

That path begins a long time ago in a galaxy far, far away. . . .

ON
THE
ICE CUBE

CHAPTER ONE

YOU GAZE out over the field of white. It is winter on the planet Hoth. It is always winter on Hoth. I mean, they have a summer. That's when the temperature crawls up to about 10 degrees below freezing. It's lovely.

It is not summer, though. It's winter, and the snow stands so deep you could lose a small child in it.

You're wearing a jacket of thick synthetic fiber, a vest on top of that, a hood, and goggles. That's the uniform of the rebels when they're out on patrol here on Hoth, riding their great Hothian tauntauns. (Those are large lizards that walk on their back feet. You know that, because you're Luke Skywalker, right? But I'm just reminding you.) All your gear doesn't insulate you from the cold, though. It is bitter and insidious. It creeps through every crack in your shell and burrows down to your bones.

Off in the distance, a meteor crashes into the snow. You squint at it. The wind whips and cracks over the ice.

"Echo Three to Echo Seven. Han, old buddy, do you read me?"

Silence. Then a crackle of static. "Loud and clear, kid. What's up?" That's Han Solo's voice. You know Han Solo, of course. But I'll just remind you: he's a space pirate, a smuggler, a scoundrel, and somewhere between your big brother and your best friend.

"I've finished my circle," you say. "I don't pick up any life readings."

Han's voice breaks through again. "There isn't enough life on this ice cube to fill a refrigerator. The sensors are placed. I'm going back."

You shiver against the wicked wind. "Right. See you soon. There's a meteorite that just hit nearby. I'm going to check it out. It won't take long."

It won't take long. Famous last words.

For it is then, just as you sign off with Han Solo, that a wampa hits you.

It rears up out of nowhere, a giant gorilla-polar-bear-abominable-snow-man-like creature. You see its tiny eyes and enormous, grinning mouth—for just an instant.

Because then its paw makes contact with your face, and your head snaps back, and the vertebrae in your neck crackle like noisemakers, and your ears are pealing like the bells in a church.

And you are in the air, flying.

Then you hit the snow.

You lie there.

Freezing.

Maybe dying.

Your tauntaun screams.

You die.

Almost.

LESSON ALPHA:
A JEDI SHOULD KNOW HOW TO COUNT

Okay. It's time for your first test.

Close your eyes.

Wait, not yet. You've got to read the instructions first.

In a moment, you're going to close your eyes. Then you're going to count, slowly, to ten.

As you're counting, try not to think about anything except the numbers.

Okay, do it now.

Did it?

Did other thoughts come into your head while you were counting? Probably. Thoughts like, "What does this have to do with being a Jedi?" and "Why is this guy so weird?" That's okay. Don't stress it.

But whenever you have a minute of quiet for the rest of today, try this again. And see if you can think *only* of the numbers. Sometimes it helps to breathe in and out on each number.

What does this have to do with being a Jedi?

A lot.

I'll explain later.

And why am I so weird?

There is no explanation for that.

CHAPTER TWO

REBEL TROOPS—soldiers, engineers, space pilots—hustle to and fro across the main hangar of the rebel base on Hoth. Han Solo stalks past, ignoring them, brushing snow from his gear.

They've been on the planet for weeks now, rebuilding their base. The Empire chased them from their last one, but they will persevere. They will continue to fight the vast and mighty Empire—and particularly the Emperor, who seems driven by the dark side itself.

Some background: the Emperor was once Senator Palpatine, of the Galactic Republic, the first government to bring lasting peace to the warring peoples of the galaxy. But Palpatine manipulated the system, gaining influence and power, until he was able to steer the Republic away from democracy and toward dictatorship—his dictatorship. During his rise to power, he ordered the execution of every Jedi. That included the Padawans, children training to be Jedi, as well.

From there, the Empire, under Palpatine's direction, set out to subdue any planet in the galaxy that did not accept his rule. Subdue, in this case, meant enslave, decimate, or entirely destroy.

So this rebel army on Hoth is the last armed resistance to the Emperor in the galaxy. Small as it is, there's nobody else.

Han Solo peers across the hangar.

Chewbacca, his longtime first mate, fiddles with the mechanics on their ship, the *Millennium Falcon*. Chewbacca is a Wookiee, which means that he's shaped like a man, but taller, and he's entirely covered with long brown hair. He looks approximately like a barbershop's floor that has stood up and is now fixing a spaceship.

Two droids pass in front of Han. The first is short and squat like a fancy trash can. He is R2-D2, the bravest service droid that Han's ever met. The second looks like the Tin Man tricked out in gold. He is C-3PO, the most cowardly, busybody protocol droid that Han has ever met. At least, that's Han's opinion.

Han is going to miss this place. The energy. The commitment to the cause. The dumb courage in the face of impossible odds. An Imperial battle station had recently destroyed an entire planet. With one shot. Han saw the debris—just bits of rock, floating in the void. You can't fight power like that.

But you can try. And this ragtag bunch of soldiers and droids, bless their foolish hearts and motherboards, are trying.

But not Han. Not anymore.

He's leaving tonight. No time for teary good-byes. No mushy stuff.

There is, though, one person that he wants to say good-bye to.

He finds her in the command center. She is

pushing buttons and barking orders into a comlink device. She looks angry. Han likes her like that.

Her name is Leia, and she is the princess of that planet the Empire destroyed with a single shot. She was on the Imperial battle station, being forced to watch. Now, she is among the leaders of the Rebellion. You can understand why.

Her brown eyes flash at the various panels and readouts. Her long brown hair is braided and wrapped in a ring around her head.

At first, Han studiously ignores her. He goes over to General Rieekan, commander of the base, who is poring over the security readouts. Like security readouts are going to help when the Empire shows up.

"General," Han says. "I'm sorry, but I can't stay here anymore."

The general looks up at Han from his readouts, gray eyes peering from under gray eyebrows. "I'm sorry to hear that." He says it like it's a question.

Han suddenly feels a bit sheepish. "Well, there's a price on my head. If I don't pay off Jabba the Hutt, I'm a dead man."

Behind Han, the princess punches some numbers into the computer. Really hard.

"You know Jabba?" Han continues. "Big, fat, ugly? Lives on Tatooine? He's no big shakes, but he knows how to shoot you in the back from halfway across the galaxy when he wants to."

The general nods sympathetically. "A death mark's not an easy thing to live with. You're a good fighter, Solo. I hate to lose you." He goes back to reading his security reports.

Han shrugs, thanks him, turns away. Toward Leia. She is punching buttons like they did something to her. He slides up beside her and whispers, "Well, your highness, I guess this is it."

"Yeah. I guess so." She mashes buttons some more. Poor buttons.

Han watches her. She refuses to look at him. He

rolls his eyes. "Well, don't get all mushy on me," he snaps. No response. He stalks off.

I am going to skip this next part, as it does indeed get kind of mushy. I will, in fact, skip all the mushy parts of the story to follow. They are neither appropriate nor relevant to a young Jedi-in-training.

All you need to know now is that Leia runs after Han, and they have an argument in which it becomes very clear that Han and Leia kind of love each other, and kind of hate each other.

When they are just at the very peak of this argument, and both are red-faced and bothered, a high and grating voice interrupts them. "Excuse me, sir!" It is C-3PO. The golden Tin Man. "Sir, oh, sir!" He sounds like a British butler with his underwear in a twist.

"Buzz off," Han replies. It's not clear whether he's talking to Leia or the golden droid.

"But, sir, I'm meant to report to you that Master Luke hasn't returned yet."

Han stops.

Leia looks at C-3PO, and then, accusingly, at Han. "He didn't come back with you?"

Han ignores her.

C-3PO continues: "He *may* have come in the south entrance, sir, but—"

"What do you mean he *may* have come in? He *may* have? *Find out!*"

Han turns to Leia and shrugs as if to say, "What can you do with these droids?"

She rolls her eyes and stalks off.

A few minutes later, Han Solo is staring out at the driving snow. The sky is a heavy gray.

"The light is fading, sir," a rebel lieutenant reports. "The temperature is dropping rapidly."

Han nods. "That's right. And my friend is out there."

Behind Han, Chewbacca is howling—Wookiees don't talk so much as make noises somewhere between those of a dog and an opera singer.

A series of beeps emanate from R2-D2. "Sir," C-3PO says, translating, "Artoo is reporting that the odds of Luke surviving out there are roughly 725 to 1."

Leia, standing behind them all, turns away.

Han zips up his coat and fixes his fur-lined hood tightly over his head.

"Sir," says the rebel lieutenant. "Your tauntaun won't make it past the first marker."

Han fixes his goggles over his eyes and climbs up on the uneasy beast. He steadies the creature, rubbing its scaly neck and whispering into its ear hole. Finally, he turns back to the lieutenant and replies, "Then I guess I'll see you all in hell."

LESSON BETA:
JEDI HAVE TO BREATHE, TOO

Second lesson. Ready?

This time, you're going to do the same thing as before, but someone else is going to count for you. Get whoever is nearby. When you close your eyes, they should silently start to count to ten. When they get to ten, have them gently tap you on the shoulder. If you have a watch or a phone that will time you, feel free to use that.

This time, when your eyes are closed, try not to have any thoughts. Just feel the air come in your nose and out of your nose. Be aware of every single breath. In and out.

Go ahead: meditate.

Did you have any thoughts, my young padawan? It's not easy to still your mind, is it? It took me many years before I could quiet my mind through meditation. But keep trying. It is the first step on the path of the Force.

CHAPTER THREE

—————————— ⊕ ——————————

YOU GROAN. Your head is pounding. Your eyes feel like they've been shut with staples. Slowly, you force them open. You blink, and blink again. A wampa is feasting on your tauntaun—*while sitting on the ceiling.* Can wampas sit on ceilings? Your temples throb.

You black out again.

Later, you wake up. The tauntaun is almost entirely eaten. The wampa, its white fur caked with blood, is no longer sitting on the ceiling. It is sitting on the floor, and you are hanging upside down. Maybe you were hanging upside down all along.

You peer up at your feet. They are trapped in ice on the ceiling. You yank at them. They do not budge.

You try to lift your body up to them, but you are too heavy, too woozy.

You stare at the blood-covered wampa. What will it eat when it's finished eating the tauntaun?

Never mind. Stupid question.

You look over the cave again, trying to ignore the wampa gnawing on your tauntaun's bones. Which is not easy.

You look past the beast.

You don't see what you're looking for.

You look behind you.

Nope.

Finally, you examine the area around you.

There it is. Half buried in snow.

Your lightsaber.

No blaster. That's probably somewhere out in the middle of a snowfield, petrifying until the end of this planet's ice age.

But that's okay. You prefer the lightsaber anyway.

It's not that far from you, so you reach for it, your arm straining in its socket, fingers grasping at the air, as if they could drag you closer. But they can't. You exhale, and let your body go limp.

The wampa is now gnawing on the tauntaun's enormous thigh bone, slurping and sucking at the supple sinews.

You look back at the lightsaber. Then you think of Old Ben. Obi-Wan Kenobi. The man who gave you the lightsaber. The man who turned your father into one of the greatest Jedi Knights of all time. The man who began to train you—before he was killed by Darth Vader. Darth Vader, the Emperor's right hand. Darth Vader, who killed your father.

You stop your mind from wandering. You focus on the lightsaber. You know what Old Ben would tell you to do.

Close your eyes. Count to ten, letting the thoughts clear from your mind. Breathe in and out. In and out. Until your mind is as empty and bright as a snowfield on a clear morning. Until you can feel everything around you. As if everything in the room has a physical shape on the field of your mind. You feel the great, hot wampa. You feel the smooth, sticky bones of the tauntaun. Then closer. The mound of snow. The lightsaber.

You touch it, in your mind. You reach out your hand. You do not strain. You just reach. You hold the lightsaber in your mind. And then, from the snowbank, the lightsaber jumps to your hand.

You open your eyes. There it is. Actually in your hand.

And there is the wampa, standing in front of you, staring at you, perplexed. And furious.

You ignite the lightsaber.

Its blade is silvery-blue. It hums, burning against the darkness. It is as serene and as powerful as the Force itself. And dangerous. Holding a lightsaber feels dangerous. At least, it does to you.

Though, right now, it's more dangerous to that blood-soaked wampa standing in front of you.

You swing the lightsaber at the ice holding your feet. You hit the ground just as the wampa lunges at you—

And its arm goes twirling across the cave.

The wampa staggers back, staring. The lightsaber is so sharp, so hot, that it has cauterized the wound. There is no blood. But there is no arm either. The great beast is in pain. And now it is afraid of you. Very afraid.

Keeping your eyes trained on the savage ice beast, your lightsaber raised high, you slowly back out of the cave.

LESSON GAMMA:
REACH OUT AND TOUCH SOMETHING— WITH YOUR MIND

You probably think that your next test will be trying to move something with your thoughts.

Yeah, we're not going to try that.

Yet.

I mean, you can give it a go. But don't be discouraged if you fail. Moving stuff with your mind is a *wee bit* difficult.

No, for this test, I want you to close your eyes—not *yet*—and breathe. It might help you to count to ten at first. Then just focus on your breath. Once you've been focusing on your breath for a while, I want you to feel what's around you. Not with your hands—with your mind. Explore the objects of the room. Your eyes should still be closed. Don't try to *remember* what's around you. Just *feel* it. Start with what you're sitting on, then anything that's in contact with your body. Work outward. What's touching those things? Feel their shapes in your mind.

Finally, I want you to focus on something near you, but that you are not touching. Trace it with your mind. Feel its shape.

Reach out. Touch it. Open your eyes.

Were you right? Was it where you thought it was? Did it look like you thought it did?

If not, don't worry. Just try it again. Remember, the most important thing is to feel everything around you. The guessing part at the end is just for fun.

CHAPTER FOUR

THE WIND IS AT GALE SPEED. Even if you knew which direction to go, you couldn't do it. The wind throws you this way and that, like you're a newspaper in a hurricane. Behind you, your trudge marks trace a crazy zigzag pattern in the mounting snow.

Your legs are shaking with strain. Your lungs are burning. Your sweaty hair is literally frozen.

You fall.

You lie, half buried in the snow. You try to rise. You fail. Your eyes close. The snow feels warm, compared to the whipping wind above. If you could just sleep for a moment or two . . . Just a little sleep . . .

(This is, of course, how you die in a snowstorm. Did you know that? Well, now you do. Never fall asleep in a snowstorm.) (See! Look at all the important things I'm teaching you!)

The minutes drift by like dreams. . . . The cold seeps through your thick thermal clothes, creeps into your skin, and then crawls along your veins,

slowly freezing them. It is coming, like an under-
taker, for your heart.

"Luke . . ."

You hear it faintly. A voice. Someone you recognize. *Go away,* you think. *I'm sleeping.*

"Luke . . ."

The voice is nearby. Maybe you should raise your

head to see who's there. But you're so tired. The cold is building a snow fortress around your heart, slowing it down.

"Luke . . ."

You decide just to go back to sleep. The cold is so gentle, and your heartbeat seems, now, so superfluous.

"Luke . . ."

The voice sounds like Old Ben's. But that's not possible. Old Ben is dead.

Unless you're dead, too . . .

And then you realize that you are dying.

Wake up! you shout at yourself. But your eyes won't open. You cannot raise your head. You are going to die.

The voice is speaking. "Luke . . . Go to the Dagobah system." It sounds like Ben. "Find my old teacher, Master Yoda . . ."

"Ben!" you cry, or try to. "Ben!" Why isn't he helping you? Where is he? You try to stay conscious, but you are failing, falling, failing, and the cold is laughing its quiet, sinister laugh. . . .

"LUKE!"

You thrust your eyes open, shattering the ice that has formed a crust over your eyelids.

Han Solo is standing above you.

"Luke, don't give up on me, kid." He is pulling you from the snow. You are hanging limply in his arms. You are trying to help him, but you literally cannot move. You've heard that Jedi can stay conscious after death, existing in the fabric of the Force. Maybe you're doing that right now. You certainly feel dead.

You suddenly become aware of a tauntaun. Good! A tauntaun is good. A tauntaun can carry you somewhere. Maybe somewhere warm, where you will be buried, because you are dead. "Han!" you say, "put me on the tauntaun." But no sound is coming out of your mouth.

And then Han's tauntaun rears back, roars to the black, snow-speckled sky, and keels over.

"Oh, great," Han mutters. He reaches over and places his gloved fingers on the beast's broad neck.

He curses. The tauntaun's heart has stopped. Now it cannot carry you to the warm place so you can be buried. You have never felt sadder in your life. You wonder if you are not a little bit loopy right now.

The scruffy space pirate looks back and forth between the lizard beast and you. Finally, he reaches over you and unhooks your lightsaber from your belt. He ignites it and looks at the tauntaun. "Sorry, old buddy," he murmurs. Then he slits the tauntaun's belly with the glowing blade. Gooey, steaming innards slide out onto the snow. "Ugh," he mutters. "And I thought they smelled bad on the outside . . ." Han lifts you from the snow and slides you into the beast's stinking belly. It feels warm and soft and smells worse than anything you have ever smelled. He is burying you! What a good friend Han is! "This isn't going to be pretty, kid," he murmurs. "But it'll keep you alive until I can get the portable shelter up."

Alive? you think. *But I'm not . . .*

And then you black out. Thankfully.

The sun rises the next morning on two snowspeeders. Their pilots scan the blinding snow with shaded eyes. "Captain Solo?" they call into their transmitters. "Commander Skywalker? Do you copy? Do you copy?"

The planet is wide, bright, and empty before them.

And then it isn't.

Their transmitters crackle to life. "Good morning!" they hear. "So nice of you to drop by!" It's Han Solo.

The pilots smile. "Echo Base, this is Rogue Two. We found them. Repeat. We found them. . . ."

LESSON DELTA:
DO SOMETHING DISGUSTING

Sometimes we have to do things that are gross.

You are at someone's home. They serve you a plate of fried kidneys. You eat it.

You are talking to a friend. She picks her nose right in front of you. You keep talking to her as if nothing happened.

You are standing beside a small cube of water. Hundreds of people have already been in this water today. Their dead skin cells are floating all over the surface. At least fourteen people have also peed in this cube of water. You dive in.

Wait. That last one is called "going to the swimming pool." That's not gross at all. That's supposed to be fun.

But why?

Shouldn't that be at least as gross as eating kidneys?

In fact, why is eating kidneys gross? You eat muscles all the time. That's called "meat." And if you eat hot dogs, you eat parts of an animal that are *way* grosser than kidneys.

All I'm trying to say is that "gross" is a matter of opinion.

In some galaxies, eating kidneys is gross. In other galaxies, swimming pools are.

As a Jedi, you can't be afraid to do something because the people around you think it's gross. You have to overcome your disgust, your fear. And everyone else's opinion. That stuff is all relative—in some places *this* is gross, in others *that* is. Be above all that.

The Force is.

Next time there's something that grosses you out, do it. Eat the kidneys. Swim in the pool. If it's not dangerous, and won't make you sick, overcome your disgust and do it.

Except picking your nose in public. Don't do that. That's gross in every galaxy.

CHAPTER FIVE

YOU'RE LYING IN BED. Down the side of your face runs a bright, angry scar. You know it's there because it makes your skin feel tight, sore. Your heart is beating slow and hard, like a jalopy that doesn't want to start.

The doors to the medical bay open, and R2-D2 rolls in, followed by a bubbling C-3PO. "Oh, Master Luke! It's so good to see you fully functional again!" C-3PO's head totters back and forth when he speaks.

"Boop beep beep beep boop boop beep boop," says the fancy trashcan.

"Artoo expresses his relief as well."

You force yourself to sit up and ignore the shooting pain in your jaw and the roaring protest of that beating knot of muscle that keeps blood flowing through your body. You gaze at these two. They're like a comedy routine, the two of them. You remember buying them on Tatooine, to help out around your uncle's moisture farm. You didn't expect R2 to have a hologram of Princess Leia, crying out for help. Nor for him to lead you to Obi-Wan. You've been through a lot with these droids. You think of them, now, as your friends.

Speaking of friends, Han saunters in from the corridor and grins at you crookedly. "How you feelin', kid?"

You shrug.

"You look okay to me. I mean, as okay as you ever have."

"Well, it's thanks to you."

"That's two you owe me."

He's right. There was a space battle with an enormous Imperial space station, not to mention a few TIE fighters, that would not have turned out so well if not for Han.

Leia's head appears in the doorway. You think of the first time you saw her, shimmering and blue and projected from R2's hologram lens. Calling for help. Calling you, though she didn't know it. There's something about her. You can't place it. But she's . . . she's really . . . something. You're not sure what.

Upon seeing Han Solo, she frowns. But then her eyes fall upon you. Her face lights up. She rushes to you and enfolds you in her arms.

But Han breaks in: "Well, Princess, it looks like you managed to keep me around a little while longer."

Leia glances disgustedly back at him. "I had nothing to do with it, and you know it. The general thinks it's too dangerous for any ships to leave the system right now."

"That's a good story . . . But I think you just can't bear to be away from a gorgeous guy like me."

You glance between them, bewildered. What's all this about?

Leia rolls her eyes. "I don't know where you get your delusions, laser brain."

Laser brain. You chuckle.

Han turns on you. "Oh, you think it's funny, kid? Well, you should have seen us alone in the south passage. She expressed her *true* feelings for me."

Leia's face has turned three shades of red. "You stuck up . . . half-witted . . . scruffy-looking . . . *nerf herder!*"

Han's eyes go wide. "Who're you calling *scruffy-looking*?!"

You have no idea what is going on. Why are your friends fighting over such stupid things?

Han's turned back to you. His words are spitting from him like bullets. "Well, it looks like I've got her all riled up, kid. You know, love is like that."

Love? you think. You are completely lost.

Leia's eyes are suddenly dangerous. "Well," she says to Han, "I guess you don't know *everything* about women." And with that, she bends down and kisses you—full on the mouth. It's warm and makes you break out in a sweat and feels weird.

And then Leia storms from the room. Han stares after her, dumbfounded. So do you.

I know, young Padawan. I promised I'd skip these mushy parts. But you'd want to know about getting kissed, wouldn't you? So you could wipe it off?

I promise, though, I'll skip any future situations like that. Probably.

Suddenly, a tinny alarm blares out of the speaker in the wall. "Foreign object breach—Marker 2. Repeat: Foreign object breach—Marker 2."

Han shakes off the scene with Leia. "Be right back, kid. You stay here."

You nod and lean back, thinking about that kiss. . . .

Two hours later, Han explodes into the medical bay.

"News?" you ask, sitting up and then instantly regretting it, as pain lances through your face.

"It's an Imperial droid," Han spits.

Suddenly, you can't feel the pain anymore. Your heart has just shifted to lightspeed. "Did it spot us?"

Han looks at the floor. "I may have blown it up."

You sit back and close your eyes.

"We're evacuating the base," Han continues. "The whole planet. We've got to go."

You sigh. It's been a good base, all things considered. But you nod. He's right. You've got to go.

LESSON EPSILON:
PEACE IS A SUPERPOWER

You've practiced meditating over the course of ten seconds. Now I want to teach you instantaneous meditation.

This is how you do it:

Close your eyes.

Smile. Gently. Don't force a smile. Just let the corners of your mouth rise.

Breathe in through your nose, deeply, until the air is all the way in the bottom of your belly.

Breathe out.

Keep smiling.

Open your eyes.

Try that.

The next time you're in a situation that makes you uncomfortable, or angry, or jealous, or so proud you think you might act like a total jerk, try this. Its effects may not last very long, but you'll feel at peace for the next few minutes.

And that might be *just* long enough to help you survive whatever it is you need to survive.

CHAPTER SIX

A N IMPERIAL STAR Destroyer is bigger than the biggest ship you've ever seen. It would take you a day to walk from one end of it to the other. A full day. That's like the size of a city. A big, bristling, flying city. With guns. Lots of guns.

The Imperial Star Destroyer that this next part of our story concerns is the largest Star Destroyer there is. The flagship. It is the second most powerful weapon in the Empire.

Yes, the second. The first most powerful weapon in the Empire is actually riding *in* the Star Destroyer. The first most powerful weapon in the Empire also wears a helmet. And breathes through an electric respirator.

The first most powerful weapon in the Empire is called Darth Vader.

You know who he is, right?

Vader was once the most promising young Jedi in the galaxy. He was Obi-Wan's student, undergoing the training that you've just begun. But he

turned to the dark side and killed his master. He is now a Dark Lord of the Sith. Which means he can do most of the cool things Jedi can do—he just does them for evil purposes.

Currently, his mission is to eradicate all resistance to the Empire.

He is, at the moment, receiving some good news.

He stands behind a group of Imperial officers: Admiral Ozzel, the upright, tradition-minded commander of the Imperial fleet; General Veers, commander of the battalion of Imperial troops tasked with eliminating the rebel army; and Captain Piett, the commander of the Star Destroyer that is currently carrying them through space.

"I think we've got something," Captain Piett is saying. "The report is only a fragment from a probe droid in the Hoth system, but it's the best lead we've had."

Admiral Ozzel shrugs off his captain. Piett is entirely too enthusiastic, in Ozzel's opinion. As if every sentence he utters might prove sufficient for a promotion. "We have thousands of probe droids searching the galaxy, Captain . . ."

"The visuals indicate life-readings, sir. And the Hoth system is supposed to be devoid of human forms."

Admiral Ozzel represses the urge to roll his eyes. These young, ambitious captains tire him so. "If we followed up every little lead a probe sent back—"

And then, Vader's voice, as deep and rich and dark as the densest black hole, cuts through the noise.

"Let me see," Darth Vader intones. He sweeps past the admiral. He wears a long black cape, and every centimeter of his skin is hidden beneath shining black metal. Vader moves toward a screen displaying a fuzzy image of buildings, and what might be a snowspeeder cruising across the ice.

"It is they," he intones. "The rebels are there."

"Lord Vader," objects Admiral Ozzel, distinctly displeased at being contradicted, "it could be anything. Smugglers, a small settlement . . ."

"It is the rebel base. I can sense it. And Skywalker is with them."

"Lord Vader . . ." Admiral Ozzel does not put much stock in Vader's "sense," nor in the hocus-pocus of "the Force" and "the dark side." Admiral Ozzel is a sensible man. A man of science and warfare.

"Set your course for Hoth, Admiral," says Vader.

In addition to not believing in all that hocus-pocus, though, Admiral Ozzel is *terrified* of Darth Vader. As is everyone.

And so the great ships of war begin to move toward Hoth.

LESSON ZETA:
YOU MUST FIND BALANCE

This time, I want you to meditate while standing on one foot.

Seems difficult, right?

Well, it should. Being a Jedi isn't easy.

If you happen to be somewhere where you can't stand on one foot, you should balance a book on your head.

If you are standing on one foot, you should keep your eyes open, and focus on a spot on the wall or the floor. Don't *look* at it. Just keep your eyes focused on it. If you're balancing the book on your head, close your eyes.

Now, count slowly to ten, focusing on nothing but the numbers.

I know that you look stupid doing this. You know you look stupid, too. But Jedi often have to do things that make them look stupid. Some people won't understand. Most people, in fact, won't understand. But if you want everyone to think you look cool all the time, you can't be a Jedi.

Jedi follow a higher calling than cool.

THE
BATTLE
FOR HOTH

CHAPTER SEVEN

THE OPPOSITE OF a Jedi Master is a Sith Lord. Well, "opposite" isn't quite accurate. Perhaps we should say a Sith Lord is the "inverse" of a Jedi Master. Or the photographic negative, where everything that is light becomes dark.

Where Jedi Masters meditate to quiet their minds and connect with the Force—that wave of energy that unifies all living things—Sith Lords meditate to concentrate their anger, their fear, and their hatred into a pure point of ruthless power within them.

This is what Darth Vader is doing, sitting in his meditation cell aboard the Empire's flagship, when General Veers enters the room. The silence is heavy. It is punctuated only by the regular breathing of the Sith Lord through his ventilator.

General Veers looks young for his position, but he has seen fire in a dozen battles. He has earned his rank through cunning and courage. He fought the Zalorians on Zaloriis. The Culroonians on Culroon III. And the Yavinians while flying through space. Backward. Never was Veers afraid.

But now, merely standing in the private chamber of Darth Vader, Veers is afraid. He remains silent. A droplet of sweat runs along a crease in his forehead.

Finally, Vader murmurs, "What is it, General?"

Even a murmur from Vader can wrong-foot a battle-hardened commander. Veers stammers before speaking. "My lord, the fleet has moved out of lightspeed. We have detected an energy field protecting an area around the sixth planet of the Hoth system. It is strong enough to withstand even our cannons."

Vader rises. His dark, looming figure looms even larger and more darkly when he is angry. "That fool of an admiral came out of lightspeed too close to the system."

"He felt surprise was wiser, Lord Vader."

"He is as clumsy as he is stupid."

Secretly, Veers agrees. But he will not reveal his opinion. He is a military man, and he knows his place.

Vader studies the clean-faced general. "Prepare for a surface attack."

The general bows and scurries from the chamber.

Vader turns to a large screen and calls up an image of Admiral Ozzel conferring with Captain Piett on the ship's bridge.

"Lord Vader," the admiral hails him, as smug as any commander on the verge of a decisive victory. "We are in position to—"

The admiral is suddenly not speaking. Rather, his mouth is moving, but no words are coming out. He searches mutely for sound—then for breath. He finds neither. His hands crawl to his neck. His eyes bulge.

"You have failed me for the last time, Admiral," Vader intones. "Captain Piett, are you there?"

A frightened captain steps around the admiral, who is now grasping at his throat frantically and turning a pale shade of blue. "Yes, Lord Vader?"

"Make ready our ships for a ground assault. You are in command now, *Admiral* Piett."

With those words, the former admiral collapses to the floor. He is dead.

LESSON ETA:
SILENCE SPEAKS LOUDER THAN WORDS—SOMETIMES

I want you to try to communicate without using your voice.

First, try communicating with only gestures. You do this all the time. You say "Hello" with a hand gesture. You say, "I'm going to the bathroom, I'll be right back," with a gesture of your hands and your face combined. You say, "If you don't let me go to the bathroom right now I am going to pee all over your floor," with your hands, face, hips, and knees. Go ahead, try that one.

Okay, now think of something you can communicate with only your eyes. You can say, "Do you agree with me?" Or, "That guy is freaking me out." Or, "I think I just peed all over your floor." Try those.

Finally, close your eyes, put your hands in your lap, and concentrate.

Try communicating with somebody nearby, using only the Force. See if you can make yourself heard, without moving a muscle.

But don't send a message about peeing on the floor. This is a waste of your Jedi powers. If you've peed on the floor, everyone will know it already.

Once the person hears you, see if you can make her actually understand you.

This isn't easy.

Being a Jedi isn't easy.

CHAPTER EIGHT

YOU'RE WEAVING THROUGH a chaos of men, women, and droids. They scramble across the rebel base, gathering up sensitive materials, readying ground weapons, and preparing transports for the evacuation. The base is as frantic as a beehive that's been kicked. Footsteps echo on the hard floor, engines fire and die and fire again. You can smell the gaseous fumes of the generators, working on overdrive to keep the shields up. The odor reminds you of your uncle's workshop on Tatooine.

To your left, Han is eyeing the lifters of his faithful ship, the *Millennium Falcon*, with guarded optimism.

"Okay, Chewie. Try it now."

Up in the spacecraft's cockpit, the Wookiee flips a switch. A spark flies from the lifters, like a blaster being fired by a drunk. Han ducks and covers his head. He straightens up, stares at his "faithful" ship balefully, and curses.

You walk up beside him. "Looks great," you say.

"Stow it, kid."

After another moment of baleful glaring, he turns away from the *Falcon*.

"Well," you nod, "take care of yourself."

"You okay to do this?" Han asks.

The effects of the cold, and of being kidnapped by a wampa, have pretty much worn off. Your heart beats like a military march now, and your senses feel quick and keen. Battle is coming. And you are ready. You tell Han all of this with just a flash of your eyes.

"Be careful out there," he says.

"You, too."

You exchange one more glance with Han. He grins at you, and nods. And in that moment you realize that, sometimes, you don't have to be a Jedi to communicate without words. Sometimes, all it takes is being friends.

In a distant wing of the rebel base, Leia is briefing a group of fighter pilots. They wear bright orange jumpsuits, like they're inmates in the coldest prison on earth. Also the coolest, because in this prison, you get to fly spaceships.

"All troop carriers will assemble at the north entrance," Leia is explaining. It's not clear who put her in charge of the X-wing briefing. But Leia's the sort of gal who doesn't need anyone's permission to take charge. "The transport ships will leave as soon as they're loaded. Only two fighters per escort."

A young pilot laughs. "Two fighters against a Star Destroyer? We're toast. Burnt toast."

Leia has a way of looking at someone that makes them feel very small and very stupid. "Thanks for your input, Hobbie. Your tactical opinions are always invaluable." The other pilots laugh. Leia goes on. "You have cover from the ion cannons on the ground. They'll clear your path." Hobbie looks at his comrades. They're nodding. "Once you pass the destroyers, get to the rendezvous point. Understood?"

"Understood!" the pilots bark. Except for Hobbie, who mutters, "This is suicide." Leia does not hear. Which is lucky. For Hobbie.

The princess dismisses the pilots and makes her way to the command center, past the hustling soldiers and engineers, the beeping droids and whirring machines. The general's old, gray eyes are scanning readings on a screen.

He knows she's there without turning around. You might say that Leia has *presence*. General Rieekan says, "The Empire has moved a destroyer directly into the path of the transports."

Leia nods. "So be it. We should let the first transport go."

The general hesitates, his eyes fixed on the Star Destroyer on the monitor. It is just one of many surrounding the planet. Beyond this cordon of ships waits one more Destroyer—the largest he has ever seen, in fact. The flagship of the Empire.

Rieekan says, "We have shoulder cannons and rocket launchers set up around the perimeter." He is almost pleading. "And Skywalker is readying a squadron of snowspeeders."

Leia's voice is a gentle rebuke. "General, you know we can't hold off the Imperial forces if they invade by ground. No matter how brave Luke is. No matter how brave any of us are. If we stay and fight, we'll be killed. We've got to launch the transports."

The general sighs, nods. His gray eyes look sad. Another base lost. Another position abandoned before the overwhelming might of the Empire. "Prepare to open the shield."

Leia turns to the shield operator. The evacuation coordinator is waiting beside him. They both wait for Leia's command. The princess merely says, "Go."

For just an instant, there is no defensive shield around the rebel base on Hoth. Three crafts—a transport and two fighters—catapult into space.

A Star Destroyer stands directly in their path.

The scene is approximately like three mice running at a tiger. The odds aren't good.

The Destroyer lowers its shields and readies its tractor beam to bring them in. The tiger is licking its lips.

The transport and two fighters approach the Destroyer.

In the rebel command center, General Rieekan

wipes his gray brow, and then dries the back of his hand on his sleeve. A droplet of sweat falls to the floor. In a moment, it has frozen.

The tractor beam locks on the transport.

The tiger's claws are out.

"Fire!" Leia bellows. A rebel ion cannon—heavy and huge and deadly and half buried in the ice of Hoth—sends two red blasts up into space, straight over the transport's bow. The blasts roar past the rebel ship and continue straight for the destroyer.

The Star Destroyer that has lowered its shields.

The ion blasts smash into the Star Destroyer's central tower. A tiny lightning storm erupts in the Destroyer's electronic epicenter, which sends shock waves out through the complex of wires that twine through the vessel like veins. The great ship pitches to one side.

The mice, it turns out, had a gun.

In the rebel command center on Hoth, a cheer erupts from every throat. The general sighs and warily eyes the princess. She is smiling at him. Reluctantly, he smiles back.

The transport and two fighters speed by the lurching Imperial ship.

LESSON THETA:
WHEN STUFF STARTS BLOWING UP

Stand on one foot, or, if you can't do that right now, balance a book on your head.

Ask someone nearby to silently, slowly, count to thirty for you.

As you balance, try to focus on nothing but your breath. Not counting. Not balancing. Just your breath, in and out, in and out.

Then, as your assistant is counting, have them clap, or shout, without warning. A few times. Can you stay balanced? Can you keep your mind still?

A still mind is necessary for being one with the Force.

Especially when stuff starts blowing up.

CHAPTER NINE

YOU AND YOUR rebel troops survey the icy field. What had once been empty, sunny, and cold as death now bristles with machines of war. Troop transports are unloading platoon after platoon of white-clad stormtroopers—the terrifying, faceless pawns of the Empire. But these the rebels can handle.

It is the snow walkers that worry you. They trudge along like motorized skyscrapers. Or maybe more like steel elephoths on stilts: four-legged, tottering hulks with cannons instead of tusks. The bright orange of your pilot's jumpsuit makes an inviting target against the snow, you realize. You wonder who decided on orange. Usually, military

uniforms are camouflage. Orange is only camouflage once you're going up in flames.

The cannons on the closest walker blaze to life,
sending bright red bursts of laser fire directly at the
rebels' trench. The ground shudders at the impact.

"Okay!" you bellow to the troops manning the
guns on the ground. "See if you can hold 'em!
Pilots, mount up!"

You open the hatch of your snowspeeder—a small
ship, outfitted with two seats inside, back to back,
for a pilot and a gunner, two laser cannons, and a
harpoon gun with a tow cable. That, in particular,
makes you feel safe. Nothing strikes more fear in
the commander of an enormous steel war machine
than a harpoon gun. Someone should have told the
designer of the snowspeeders that these elephoths
are made of steel.

Your gunner, young and fresh-faced, climbs in
behind you.

"Hey, Luke," he says. "Feeling better?"

"Like new, Dak. You?"

Young Dak turns around to shoot you a brave smile. "I feel like I could take on the whole Empire by myself."

"I know what you mean." You grin. Still, looking at Dak, you notice his downy cheeks are pale and drawn. And for good reason. Every rebel on Hoth won't be enough to rebuff this small contingent of Imperial troops. Not nearly enough. Dak knows it, and so do you.

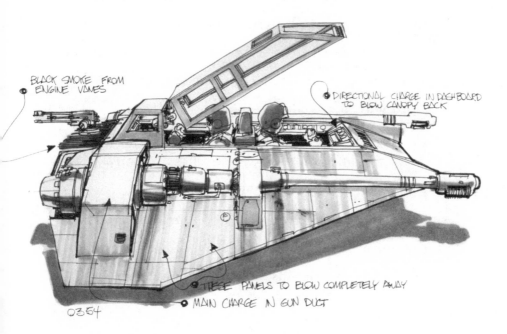

BLACK SMOKE FROM
ENGINE VANES

DIRECTIONAL CHARGE IN DASHBOARD
TO BLOW CANOPY BACK

THESE PANELS TO BLOW COMPLETELY AWAY
MAIN CHARGE IN GUN DUCT

0354

Nevertheless, within minutes you and the other speeders are flying across the quilted ice, locked in on the hulking behemoths of war.

"All right, boys, stay together now . . ." you call.

Dak's high voice is shaky: "Luke, I can't get a read on them."

So you say, "Steady, Dak."

You lead the speeders into an attack formation.

Two blasts explode just off the speeder's starboard side. You bank hard right, circumnavigating the explosion and flying out wide to the beast's flank, where its great tusk-like guns can't hit you. Then you kick up the accelerator and aim at its legs. "You with me, Dak?"

"I'm okay, sir." He doesn't sound okay.

From the trenches in front of the base, rebel fire keeps the platoons of stormtroopers at bay, preventing them from rushing the power generators. This is the point of the whole attack. No power generators, no shields. No shields, and those Star Destroyers up in the sky scorch the rebel base into oblivion.

But the rebel fire is doing nothing to slow the snow walkers, which are lumbering inexorably onward, laser blasts bouncing uselessly off their armor.

Your craft approaches the lead snow walker. Another speeder skims the snow just behind you.

Then it explodes. "They got Rogue Seven!" Dak yells.

You grit your teeth. "Stay with me, Dak. We're coming in." The speeder darts between the snow walker's tall, double-jointed legs. "Now!"

Dak might be nervous, but those young hands are steady. His blast explodes directly on the under-side of the walker's head.

Your stomach turns over.

The walker is moving forward. Entirely unaffected.

"Forget the blasters!" you shout into the inter-com. Other pilots are cursing.

You pause. And then you think of elephoths.

"Use your harpoon and tow cables! Go for their legs!"

A pilot's voice crackles through the transmitter. "Will that work?" Lasers are exploding all around him.

"No idea! But the blasters won't!"

"Luke!" Dak's voice is laced with panic now. "Luke! We've got a malfunction in the fire control!"

"Hold on, Dak. Focus on the tow cable!"

"Luke!"

"Stay focused!" You're steering toward another snow walker, through a crushing volley of lasers and shrapnel.

You're getting closer. The snow rushes beneath the ship; the great beast is growing before you. The sounds of explosions, crunching snow, and buckling metal are nearly deafening.

"Ready, Dak?"

There is no response.

"Dak?" You turn around.

Dak's head is slumped over to one side, and his body lies limp against a blinking control panel. Blood is clotting in his hair.

You swivel back to your steering columns. You feel sick.

You take a deep breath. Your eyes are open, but you do not see. You are breathing, in and out, in and out.

Dak is dead.

Yes, and you cannot change that.

LESSON IOTA:
PEACE IN A TIME OF CRISIS

What? Meditate? Luke's gunner—and friend—is dead, and he's supposed to *meditate*?

Yup.

I mean, he could give in to rage or despair. Go out in a blaze of glory. Or turn tail, run, seethe, weep.

Those would all be normal things to do.

But those are, at best, the paths to defeat. At worst, they are paths to the dark side.

Think of something that has upset you, my young friend. Something that makes your blood race through your veins, or brings up an uncomfortable bulge in your throat when you think of it. When someone teased you, or lied to you, or hurt you. Please—think back to such a time.

Now stand on one foot, or balance the book on your head, and breathe. Have someone count to thirty, or time yourself. See if you can focus only on your breath. Nothing else.

Did it?

It isn't easy, is it?

Go ahead: keep trying. You're making progress. I can tell.

CHAPTER TEN

THE SNOW WALKERS are nearing the rebel trench. Behind the trench, a dish gazes up into the sky. In great cubes of steel and lithium, power surges, flowing to the halls of the rebel base, to the ion cannons, to the shields.

Your breath is flowing in and out of your body. Your eyes are clear. You are calm. You speak: "Rogue Leader to Rogue Three, I've lost Dak. You'll have to take this shot. Follow me on the next pass."

"Coming round, Rogue Leader."

The speeders bank, and you steer for the legs of the lead snow walker. Your hands grip the steering column, knuckles blanching with the pressure, breath concentrated into a single line that goes in your nose, down to the bottom of your belly, and then gently flows out the way it came. Laser blasts erupt all around you. You ignore them. They will not hit you. You can tell.

You reach the snow walker, and as you duck through its great legs, followed hard by Rogue Three, you shout, "Go!"

From the back of Rogue Three, a harpoon shoots out and buries itself in the snow walker's knee joint.

You turn hard, creating a tight circle around the snow walker. Rogue Three follows. You peel off, but Rogue Three continues its run, looping the steel tow cables around and around and around the snow walker's legs. At last, Rogue Three follows you away from the steel beast.

"Release!" the pilot shouts. His gunner obeys, and the tow cable detaches from the speeder as it retreats, screaming over the snow.

As you speed away, the enormous snow walker attempts another step toward the trench and the power generators behind it. It lifts its great foreleg— and then stutters. The war machine totters, just for

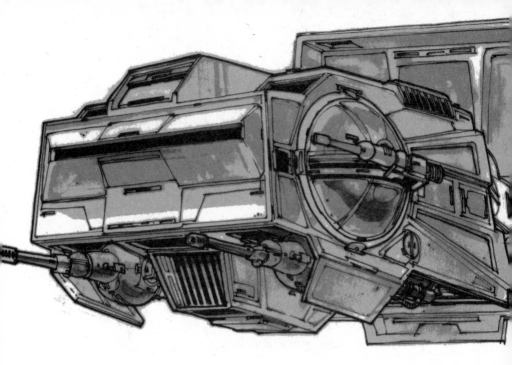

a second. And then, like a great tree after a lumber-jack calls "Timber!" it tumbles through the air and smashes into the ground with a gruesome shudder. It will not rise again.

But the assault continues. Blast after blast, from snow walkers and rocket launchers, rock the rebel base.

Han Solo rushes through the smoky halls, fol-lowed by a panicked C-3PO. He finds his way, through the shouting and the drifts of smoke and the smell of burning plastic, to the command center. There, Leia is commanding the general. Han almost smiles. Her throat is straining, her voice ragged with shouting.

"We have to launch the last transports now! Both of them! This is the end!"

"We can't cover two at once . . ." General Rieekan is pleading with her.

Leia's cheeks are red like hot steel, and her eyes are just as bright. "We have to try!" Then she turns and sees Han. She jabs a finger at him through the air. "What are you still doing here? You had clearance to leave!"

"Don't worry, I'll leave. But I've got to get you to your ship. You'd stay way past the end if I didn't. . . ." Han says it like it's criticism. But it isn't.

"Your Highness!" C-3PO warbles frantically. "We must take one of the final transports! It's our last hope!"

Leia pivots to the grey-eyed general. "Send all troops in sector twelve to protect the soldiers on—"

Gravity goes funny. The ground is shifting beneath them. C-3PO careens into Han, his golden arms scrabbling at the air. One strikes Han in the face. Han grabs the tumbling droid and steadies him.

A voice comes over the general address system. "Imperial troops have entered the base. Repeat. Imperial—"

"That's it, Princess," says Han, taking her arm. "We're going."

"Signal total evacuation!" Leia shouts to the general, as Han drags her away. "And get to your transport!"

Han leads Leia into the corridor. Red lights are ablaze everywhere. C-3PO totters behind, still babbling frantically. Shouts and cries compete with desperate announcements over the loudspeaker to which no one is listening. Occasionally, an explosion drowns the rest of it out. The smoke smells now not only of plastic and metal, but of flesh. The rebels have lost. They have lost.

Another explosion rocks the corridor, and this time, the ceiling falls in. Right in front of them.

Leia stares at it, bewildered. But just for an instant. Then she falls upon the rubble, trying to clear it from their path. But there's too much, and it's piled too high. Han watches her, frozen. The explosions are getting closer. Then he pulls his transmitter to his mouth. "Transport, this is Solo. I've got the princess with me. I can't get to you. I'll get her out on the *Falcon*."

Leia turns from the rubble. "That bucket of bolts can't get past the blockade!"

"That's your ride, Princess," Han calls back over his shoulder as he starts down the hall, away from the rubble, C-3PO tottering behind. "It's up to you!"

Leia hesitates. She looks down the blocked corridor. She glances after Solo. "We'll never survive!" she shouts.

And he shouts back, "At least we'll never survive together!"

She frowns, hesitates, and runs after him.

The once-peaceful snow plain is now streaked and stained with blood and oil, shrapnel and space junk. The air, once whistling only with the wind, now whistles with laserfire and crashing ships.

You bank your speeder for another run at a snow walker.

"Rogue Two, are you all right?"

"I'm with you, Rogue Leader."

"Your harpoon this time. I'll cover you with my manual blasters."

"Like hunting sharwhales on Uthura! I'm coming home!" the pilot of Rogue Two crows.

You laugh. "Okay, don't get too far out ahead of me now."

But Rogue Two isn't listening. Taken by adrenaline and fear, he's already shot out onto the icy expanse between you and the walker.

"Slow down!" you tell him.

"Rogue Two, coming home!"

And then he explodes.

From across his bow, a bright red blast of laser hits his speeder directly in its propulsion system.

You watch in horror. And in that moment—as you stare at that brave pilot with the stupid sense of humor smoldering in the wreckage of his speeder, his gunner desperately trying to pry himself out of the back—that's when you're hit.

The control panel looks like a thunderstorm. Your dials are spinning, readouts have become tiny electric light shows. You're trying to hold the ship up, but gravity is fighting a battle with your speeder, and suddenly, it's winning. The g-force is strong, and stronger, and you are pulling up—but that's not doing a thing. Your head is being flattened into your seat. You lock your jaw and close your eyes.

The ship slams into the ice.

You cannot breathe.

Do you know the feeling? When you get the wind knocked out of you?

You gasp at the air, but it will not enter your mouth. You arch your back, desperate, empty, literally breathless. Screaming in silence for the breath that just moments ago you never had to think about.

And then the wind comes rushing back into your lungs, and you thank the Force, or whatever you believe in, and you breathe.

You breathe, just as the enormous steel foot of a snow walker appears over your tiny snowspeeder.

You gaze up at it, motionless. The steel foot descends. You will be crushed. You will be crushed, and you will die.

And then the cockpit is open, and you are over the metal gunwale, and you are rolling, rolling, rolling—a child's game turned suddenly serious— rolling across the icy snow. The great foot crashes down upon the speeder, and the snow walker continues its inexorable march toward the rebel base.

You spring to your feet. You don't know where you get the energy. It courses through you, though, like your newly regained breath. You start to run.

At full speed, you can just keep pace with the war machine. You look over the ruined field of snow, the sun hanging bright and distant in the empty blue sky. The rebels in the trench are barely firing anymore. They must be retreating, back to the transports. It's over. Their only hope now is to get out before the power generator is destroyed, and the shields go down, and the great armada of Star Destroyers hovering just out of orbit pulverizes the base with their cannons—obliterating it and everyone inside. The only question now is how soon those generators will be blown. The sooner they are, the more rebels will die.

Still running, you look up at the steel under-belly moving above you. Swinging from your belt is a harpoon gun. For elephoth hunting, you think.

Ridiculous to carry it into battle. But it's standard rebel equipment. Lucky for you.

You aim it upward and let it fire. It catches on a mechanism on the snow walker's underbelly, its steel cable trailing back to your hand. Running sideways now, you fasten the cable to your belt and hit "retract" on the gun. Suddenly, you are careening upward through the air, toward the belly of the walker. Your arms and legs dangle, your belt is trying to tear itself from your body, and the wind is so cold on your neck that your teeth hurt. You reach for your lightsaber. The belly approaches. It arrives. You are dangling like a spider. A deadly spider.

With a single swing, you hew the hinges from the escape hatch in the belly of the steel beast. The door goes spinning down into the snow.

In a pouch hanging from the back of your belt is a grenade. You don't like grenades. If you want to commit the dire and irreparable act of taking a life, you think, you ought to at least look the person in the face before you do it. That is why Jedi prefer lightsabers. Also, it is harder to kill someone accidentally with a lightsaber. Grenades, like guns, have a disturbing tendency to take the life of the wrong person.

But you're not a Jedi Knight. Not yet. You're just a kid with a lightsaber. Maybe you would be a Jedi already, if Darth Vader hadn't killed Old Ben. Rage grabs your shoulders and chest, making them tight and hot. You wonder if Vader is out on one of those Imperial Star Destroyers, waiting to kill you, too.

Old Ben. What had he said, while you lay unconscious in the snow? Dagobah? Yoda? *Master* Yoda?

The snow walker fires a blast right at the satellite dish perched on the generator. It bursts into flames. *Focus!* you tell yourself. You start the detonation sequence on the grenade and hurl it through the hatch. Then you release the cable from your belt.

As you hurtle snow-ward, you suddenly wonder if the walker will crash down on you when it explodes.

LESSON KAPPA:
RELAX! PEOPLE ARE SHOOTING AT YOU!

Get someone to help you.

You are going to stand on one foot, or balance that book on your head, and someone is going to—very gently—throw things at you. These things should be soft. I recommend balled up socks or crumpled pieces of paper. They should be thrown gently. You are going to bat them away with your hands without losing balance.

Get yourself set—stand on one foot or put the book on your head. Do one second of instantaneous meditation—close your eyes, smile, breathe in and out, open your eyes. Then have your assistant begin to gently toss objects at you.

See if you can stay balanced and still defend yourself.

Get going, young one. Let's see what you've got.

CHAPTER ELEVEN

---◈---

"**A**AAARRAAARAAGH!" An enormous, opera-singing dog yodels soulfully beside the *Millennium Falcon*. No, wait. That is Chewbacca. Never mind.

"Aaaarraaaraagh!" Chewbacca howls mournfully. His small eyes dart from the *Millennium Falcon* to the hangar doors. They will remain open another few minutes. At most. After that, the *Falcon* will not fly, no matter if the walking barber-shop floor succeeded in fixing the lifters or not.

"Araararararargh!" he cries again. Not that the Wookiee minds dying. Not really. Wookiees are nothing if not valiant. But they are also fiercely loyal. Chewbacca is not worried for himself. He's worried for Han, and for Leia.

Just then, they come sprinting around a corner.

"Aarararararargh!" That is Chewbacca, howling joyfully. In case you couldn't tell the difference.

Han shouts, "Start 'er up, Chewie! Start 'er up!"

Chewie leads the way up the gangplank, followed by Han and Leia. C-3PO totters into view around a distant corner. "Oh, wait! Wait for me!"

He should hurry. They will absolutely not wait for him.

Well, maybe Leia would.

In the cockpit, Han throws switches all over the place. Chewbacca studies the readings skeptically. Han glances at his first mate, who growls in the negative.

Leia leans over Han's shoulder. "Would it help if I got out and pushed?"

"It might."

"Sir," says C-3PO, "might I suggest . . ."

Han raises a single eyebrow at the droid. "Ah, never mind," C-3PO concludes sheepishly.

The captain leaps from his seat. He rushes from

control panel to mechanical bank back to control panel.

Leia puts her hands on her hips. "This jalopy will never get past the blockade."

"Oh, she's got some surprises left in her, sweetheart."

"Don't call me that."

"I was talking to the ship."

Outside the *Falcon*, a power gasket explodes.

"Aaaarraaaraagh!" Chewbacca roars. Not joyfully.

"I'm trying!" Han shouts "I'm trying!"

Suddenly, in the space of the hangar door, stormtroopers appear.

"Now it's a party!" Leia shouts.

One of the stormtroopers mounts a rocket launcher on his shoulder.

As Han fiddles with some wiring under the cockpit's main dash, Leia slides into the captain's seat and fires at the stormtroopers. They are sent hurtling through the air in six different directions. Then she gets out of the seat. Han looks up at her for a moment, not sure if she's moved or not, and then goes back to furiously fiddling with wires.

"Now!" he shouts at Chewbacca. The Wookiee pulls back on a thruster, and the *Falcon* roars to life.

"Woo-hoo!" Han cries, leaping into the captain's chair.

"One day," Leia says, "you're going to be wrong. I just hope I'm there to see it."

Han Solo flashes her a smile. The hangar doors begin to close.

"Punch it!" Han shouts. Chewbacca throws a switch, and the *Millennium Falcon* roars out of the rebel base, up through the snowy sky of Hoth, and into the blackness of space.

You hit the snow. It explodes around you. The snow walker lumbers ahead three, four, five steps. You are breathing hard, watching it go. The rebel troops have fled the trench. The fight is over. The snow walker fires at the generators. One catches fire.

Then, overhead, you see it: Han's rickety old ship,

still supposedly "the fastest in the galaxy," shoots out of the south hangar and climbs up through the atmosphere. You smile. At least Han got out. Hopefully the princess, too. Yes. She's in that ship. You can tell.

And then an explosion presses you into the ground. A wave of heat courses over your body. You are lying on your back, the snow rapidly melting around you, fire licking your chest. Then it subsides. You raise the blackened visor of your helmet. The snow walker is dangling from its own legs, a blackened husk.

You get up and run.

On a remote part of the ice field, far away from the battle and the now-ruined rebel base, you trudge through the snow. A short distance farther sits your X-wing, a spaceship outfitted for one pilot and one droid. R2 is in his place. He's the one who piloted it out here to the muster site, to wait for you. The last of the other pilots are taking off, leaving a strange sight: a spaceship, small and lonesome, sitting on the edge of a frozen wilderness. The sounds of battle seem very distant out here.

You hoist yourself into the cockpit.

"Beep boop boop beep!"

You grin. "Hi, Artoo. Everything okay?"

"Boop beep beep, beep boop boop."

"Aw, that's sweet. I'm fine. I just hope everyone else is."

You punch some numbers into the X-wing's navigation system.

"Beep boop boop boop boop!" R2 objects.

"I know. We're not meeting them at the rendezvous point."

"Boop beep beep beep?"

"No. We're going somewhere else."

"Boop beep beep?"

"It's called Dagobah."

"Boop beep boop."

"I'd never heard of it either. But there's someone there I need to meet."

"Beep?"

"He's called Yoda." You initiate the engine.

"Beep boop boop boop."

"Well, some people might say that Artoo-Detoo is a stupid name, too," you retort.

"Beep beep beep beep? Beep boop boop boop, beep beep."

"It's just something I have to do, Artoo. Just something I have to do."

STRANGE
PLANETS
PART I

CHAPTER TWELVE

YOUR X-WING HOVERS over an emerald
planet. It is a shimmering green orb, with
large patches of blue, indicating, perhaps,
great inland lakes. Clouds and mist swirl
over the planet's surface like steam rising from a
cauldron.

"I'm not picking up any cities or technology, Artoo," you say. "Massive life-form readings,
though. There's something alive down there. A lot
of somethings, actually."

"Boop beep beep boop boop."

"No, I'm not going to change my mind. I'm
going to find this Yoda."

"Boop beep beep beep."

"Artoo! Watch your language!"

The ship descends through the atmosphere, submerging itself deeper and deeper into the swirling mist and cloud. You can't see a thing. An alarm sounds in the cockpit. R2 beeps at you. "I know!" you shout. Your eyes frantically scan the scopes and meters. They're all dead.

You get the strangest notion in your head. It's as if you're descending into some kind of dream, a place where technology doesn't work, where science and logic fail. You try to shake the thought away— and then the ship shakes you back. Hard. You're being pushed back into your seat. Cracking and snapping echo through the cockpit, but the mist is so thick and deep you can't tell if it's the ship breaking or whatever's outside.

The X-wing is falling, plunging, deeper and deeper into the dreamworld.

Your neck snaps forward as the ship jerks to a stop.

Your head is pounding. Woozily, you try to make

out the readings from the X-wing. There are no readings. The ship is no longer functioning at all.

Wherever you've just landed, you're not leaving anytime soon.

You are now standing on the very threshold of your training.

You have come to a place halfway between waking and dreaming, between the physical and the mystical.

Welcome to Dagobah.

LESSON LAMBDA:
STRANGE PLACES, NEW WORLDS

I want you to do something dangerous. Not *too* dangerous—don't die on me, kid. But something outside your comfort zone. Something that makes your skin tingle, just a little bit.

Think of a place that you haven't gone before. It can be nearby. Maybe it's the janitor's closet in your school. Maybe it's the basement of your public library (look around, it has one). Maybe it's your own attic, at night, when everyone's sleeping. Someplace that's a little strange, a little creepy.

Next chance you get, go there. Alone. Don't tell anyone what you're doing. Slip into that strange place, close the door behind you (don't let it lock—starving to death counts as dying on me), and sit there. Maybe you're in darkness. Maybe you're not. Explore the place, with your mind, with your hands. Be alone there.

Do you feel scared?

Good. You should be.

CHAPTER THIRTEEN

───────────────── ✦ ─────────────────

YOU ARE STANDING on the hull of your X-wing. It is half submerged in swamp. You can barely see. The air is dark and thick, and mists drift by, enveloping you in a warm cocoon of dew.

You are afraid. There is life on this planet—the place teems with it. Some of it is poisonous. Some of it is sharp-toothed. Some of it is slow and strong and hungry. And you can't see any of it.

There's a splash. "What's that?" you whisper. "Artoo?"

No response.

"Artoo?"

Just the burbling, steaming silence of the darkness answers your call.

"Artoo!"

You rush to the side of your ship. Suddenly, the X-wing lurches beneath you. You stick out your arms, sway, and steady yourself. R2 is gone. Ripples radiate out into the swamp.

Frantically, you scan the morass, squinting into the murky gloom. "Artoo! Artoo-Detoo!"

If there are hungry creatures about, they know you are here now—if the crashing of the ship hadn't told them, your screaming has. They know exactly where you are. Unfortunately, you don't know where they are.

Suddenly, R2's periscope appears above the surface of the swamp. You sigh. "Get to land," you call. "No telling what's in that swamp with you—" You stop speaking.

The black back of a large creature breaches the surface of the swamp. Just behind R2-D2. Then it dives. Gone.

You stare, as decisive as a weather vane in a cyclone. R2's periscope is making its slow way to the nearest bank. Surely, the creature's not interested in eating a hunk of circuits and metal. This is what you tell yourself. But your hands are sweating.

R2 has reached the bank. His rounded dome of a head emerges from the water, followed by his cylindrical body. You begin to exhale.

Which is when the creature takes him.

"Artoo!" you scream.

He's gone, sucked back into the swamp. The water, already turbid, churns with the struggle.

"Artoo! Fight him! Come on, Artoo!" Forget the other predators lurking nearby. You'll scream for R2. He might be a droid, but he's your friend. You'd fire your blaster, but you'd be just as likely to hit the little droid. And your lightsaber won't reach. Not nearly. So you just shout. "Fight him!"

The water falls still. You stare. A bead of sweat drips from your nose.

"Artoo?" you murmur.

And then R2-D2 is flying up out of the swamp, screaming his shrill whistling scream. He crashes into the trees, some thirty yards from the bank.

You bound over the X-wing's hull and leap to safe ground. You dash to him. He's lying on his back, tangled in branches and vines and roots, covered with swamp mess. You try to brush him off. He smells disgusting. But you can't help smiling.

"Good thing you taste so bad," you tell him.

His response is *not* polite.

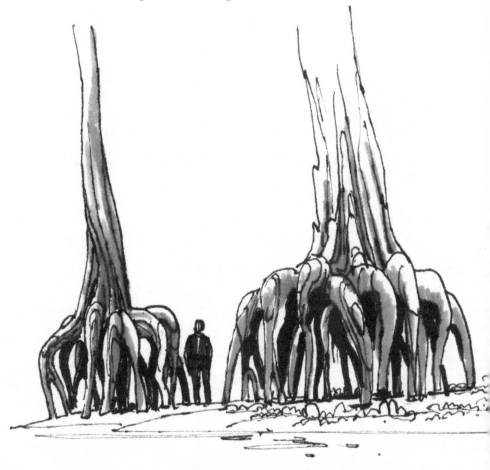

You're sitting amid boxes on the bank of the swamp. You've plugged R2 into his power regenerator. You've rescued your premade shelter from the X-wing and placed most of the components where they should go, and you've opened your rations box. You gnaw on a protein stick, watch your ship sink slowly into the bog, and think about how useless, how indecisive you were, when R2 was getting eaten by that swamp thing. You feel sick. Then you think of Leia and Han and Chewie—and even C-3PO—in that flying hunk of bolts. Last you saw them, they were heading straight toward an Imperial armada. You didn't help them. Just like you didn't help R2. You flew off to this planet to find some name from some hallucination you had. Yoda? There's no Yoda. You pick up a stick and start breaking it.

"What are we doing here, Artoo?"

"Beep beep beep boop boop beep. Beep beep beep."

"Maybe I *should* have listened to you. Ben told me Master Yoda was here." You stare around at the overgrown fen. The whole place smells of rot. "What Jedi Master would live *here*? There's not even a spaceport. . . ."

"*Spaceport?* What is spaceport?"

You leap to your feet and spin at the same time, hands raised in self-defense.

Half a meter from you sits one of the strangest creatures you have ever seen. He's bluish-green, with long ears and bulging eyes. Your hand creeps slowly toward your lightsaber. "Who are you?" you demand.

"I ask question first!" the creature laughs. His voice is raspy and high—as if a frog had learned to talk. Maybe he *is* some kind of frog. Then you think, *No, his ears are too big.*

Before you've registered it, he is rummaging through your food. "Food this is?" he croaks. "Hungry I am!"

"Get out of there! That's mine!"

"What is yours?" he asks, chewing on one of

your dehydrated veggie bars and then throwing it away.

"That is!"

"What is mine?" he continues, as if you'd interrupted him. "Yours and mine is not. There only is."

"What? Stop talking nonsense! Get out of here!"

R2-D2, who's been beeping madly since this little gnome showed up, is reaching his long, retractable arm out to grab a protein stick that the creature has begun to nibble on. He gets hold of it. The creature refuses to let go. They start a tug-of-war over the protein stick.

"Where am I?" you mutter, staring at the surreal scene. The creature has picked up a gnarled walking stick and is hitting R2-D2 over the head with it as he desperately grips the protein stick with his free hand.

"Oh, just let him have it, Artoo!"

R2 lets go and goes tumbling backward.

The creature sits down and with a satisfied grin

takes a bite of the protein stick. Suddenly, he con-
torts his strange face into an even stranger one and
throws the stick over his shoulder. "How get so big,
do you, eating such bad food?"

"It's not meant for little swamp frogs," you reply.
"It's meant for humans."

The creature peers up at you. "What are you
doing here, I am wondering?"

You sigh. "I'm looking for a great warrior."

"Great warrior, you say? War makes not one
great."

You shake your head. You can barely make sense
of what he's saying. "Fine. I'm looking for a great
Jedi Master, then."

"A Jedi Master? Yoda you want!"

You perk up. "You know him?"

"Know him I do. Take him to you I can. But
first, eat we must! Come!" The little creature picks
up the gnarled stick he'd been hitting R2 with and
uses it as a cane. Not that he needs one. He bounds
over roots twice his height with apparently little

effort. You struggle behind him, sweat dripping down your hair and into your eyes, the rich, fetid smell of the swamp clogging your nostrils. R2 rolls and totters behind you—sometimes. The rest of the time you have to carry him.

Your shirt is soaked and your back is aching when the little frog creature comes to a stop. You put R2 down with a grunt. You are standing before what looks like a pile of roots and mud that someone cut a single door and window into. "This is where Yoda lives?"

"My house this is! Eat we must!"

The door's so low you have to crawl through it. R2 can't even fit, so you tell him to wait outside. He peers through the single round window and mutters low beeps and whistles. You hope the creature can't understand them. You've known space pirates who wouldn't use the language R2 does.

Once in the house, the creature immediately busies himself with cooking. He has a pot hung over a little fire, and two small cauldrons sitting among coals, and he runs back and forth between them, throwing roots and swamp weed into them. As he cooks, the smell that wafts through the room reminds you of a garbage depot in the hot season on Tatooine.

Then you sense it. Something is moving behind you. You glance back—and dive to the ground. There is a very large snake. Or maybe it's not a snake. It could be a slug. A slake, maybe. Or a snug. Whatever it is, it gives you the creeps. You glance between the snlug and the blue-green crea-

ture. He doesn't pay any attention to it. You find another seat. The little frog-man bustles over the putrid meal, humming to himself, as outside R2 mumbles a stream of electronic invective so foul you're blushing. Finally, you can't take it any longer. "When am I going to see Yoda?" you blurt.

"Later! Later! Now we eat! Even Jedi Master is eating now!"

The creature shoves a spoonful of root-leaf stew into your mouth. It has the consistency of boiled brains, and you're about to spit it out when you stop—it doesn't taste terrible, actually. You chew and swallow.

"Good? Good!" squeals the little creature.

"Yes," you say, surprised. "Good. Can I see Yoda now?"

"First," says the creature, "a story I tell!"

"What? No!"

"Short story. Good story. You sit. You listen. Maybe learn something you will. About Yoda."

You sigh. If you'll learn something about the Jedi Master, maybe it's worth hearing the story. You settle yourself among the roots, coals, and steaming pots—making sure no more snakes are sharing your seat. The ceiling is low and smoky above you. The smell of boiling swamp-weed suffuses the little house. The light is dim and red.

The creature begins.

Now, I'm going to tell you the creature's story as I've heard it, passed down through the years. I'm not going to try to replicate the creature's strange way of speaking. Besides, you wouldn't know what I was talking about. *I* wouldn't know what I was talking about. I'm just going to tell it. It goes like this:

A long time ago in a galaxy far, far away, there lived a poor man with his three sons.

The oldest son was strong and handsome and everyone thought he was very wonderful. He agreed with them.

The second son was wise and clever, and everyone thought he, too, was very wonderful. He also agreed with them.

The youngest son was quiet and thoughtful and everyone thought he was an idiot. He did not agree with them. But nobody cared what he thought.

One day, the oldest son announced that he was going out into the wide world to find his fortune.

His father begged him not to go. "Stay and help your poor father on the farm! If you go, who will milk the cow and feed the chickens? We'll all starve!"

But the oldest son said, "My brothers can milk the cow and feed the chickens! I'm off to seek my fortune!" So he packed a bag with plenty of food for his journey, and off he went.

Soon, he came to a dark and frightening forest. He hesitated, just beyond the forest's shadows. And then he saw, sitting by the side of the path, a toad.

The toad croaked at him. "Hungry I am! Share your food with me, will you?"

(Yes, I realize the toad talks like the creature on Dagobah. I don't know why. That's just the way the story's always told.)

But the brother refused. "Begone, you filthy toad! I am off to seek my fortune!" He tried to kick the toad, and then he strode forward into the dark wood.

Soon he came to a great palace. Its walls were as tall and strong as tree trunks, and banners waved from every turret. The boy wanted to know who lived in such a castle, so he asked one of the guards. The guard said it was a great king.

"Perhaps this king will make me the commander of his army!" the oldest son exclaimed. "Take me to him!"

So he was brought before the king. The king sat on a simple throne, and he wore no crown. When the boy saw the king, he announced, "I have come to seek my fortune!"

"Your fortune you seek?" replied the king. "Then your fortune you shall have!"

And with those words, the oldest brother was suddenly transformed into a fly. A long tongue shot out from the king's mouth, caught the oldest brother, and pulled him down the king's throat.

The creature peers up at you, as if expecting you to speak.

"That was a good story," you say. Really, you're just trying to be polite. You begin to stand up. "Can I see Yoda now?"

The creature growls, "Finished it isn't! Listen you must. Interrupt do not, or take you to Yoda I won't!"

You frown and force yourself to listen. The toadlike creature continues his strange tale.

Back at the poor man's house, the second brother and the youngest brother worked twice as hard to milk the cow and feed the chickens and care for their poor father.

But after some time, the second son announced that he was going out into the wide world to find his fortune, just like his brother had.

His father begged him not to go. "Stay and help your poor father on the farm! If you go, who will milk the cow and feed the chickens? We'll starve!"

But the second son said, "My brother can milk the cow and feed the chickens! I'm off to seek my fortune!" So he packed a bag with plenty of food for his journey, and off he went.

He followed the same road as the oldest brother, and soon he came to the same dark forest. He, like his brother, hesitated just beyond the wood's shadows. And then he saw, sitting by the side of the road, a cat.

"Hungry I am," the cat said. "Share your food with me, will you?"

(Yes. The cat also talks like the creature. Again, I have no idea why.)

But the second brother also refused. "Begone, you mangy cat! I am off to seek my fortune!" He tried to kick the cat, and then he strode forward into the dark wood.

Soon he came to the same great palace, and he, too, asked who lived there. The guard said it was a great king.

"Perhaps this king will make me his closest adviser!" the second son exclaimed. "Take me to him!"

So he was brought before the king. When the boy saw the king, he announced, "I have come to seek my fortune!"

"Your fortune you seek?" replied the king. "Then your fortune you shall have!"

And with those words, the second brother became a mouse. And the king reached out with a great paw and crushed the brother. And then the king ate him up.

You are watching the little creature tell his tale. You have noticed something in him—something you had not seen before. Intensity. Age. And some hidden, ferocious force.

You cannot put a name to it.

But it scares you.

Back at the poor man's house, the youngest brother worked three times as hard to milk the cow and feed the chickens and care for his poor father.

But one day, the youngest brother came before his father and said, "Father, I would like to go out into the world and discover what has happened to my two brothers."

His father begged him not to go. "You are just a simple boy. You will be lost . . . or worse. Stay here and milk the cow and feed the chickens and take care of your poor old father."

But the youngest son said, "I have set aside ten pails of milk for you to drink and a hundred eggs for you to eat, for my brothers are gone and there is plenty of extra food now. Eat what I have set aside for you, and I promise I will return before it is all gone." When the father saw what his youngest son had done, he agreed to let him go.

So the boy packed a bag with a little bit of food and set down the same road as his brothers had. And soon, he came to the same dark forest. He, like his brothers, hesitated just beyond the wood's shadows. And then he saw, sitting by the side of the road, a chicken.

"Hungry I am," the chicken said. "Share your food with me, will you?"

So the youngest brother sat down and opened his bag, and laid out all the food he had brought for his journey on the ground. And he and the chicken sat and ate. The chicken had an enormous appetite, and soon all the food was gone.

Then the brother picked up his bag and ventured into the dark forest. His stomach began to rumble, but his bag was empty. Kilometers and kilometers he went, until his legs were shaking and he was on the verge of collapsing from hunger.

Just when he thought he could go no farther, he came to the castle in the wood. He asked the guard who lived there, and heard it was a great king. "Perhaps the king knows where my brothers are!" he said. "May I see him?" He was so weak with hunger that he had to be carried up to the king's throne room.

When the boy saw the king, he fell to his knees. "Please, king, help me. I seek my brothers, who ventured into this wood and disappeared. Also," he added, "I am very hungry."

The king laughed, and his laugh sounded like this: "Buck-buckaw!"

Then the king said, "Brothers you shall not see. Dead they are. But this chicken feed you must take. To your father's chickens you will give it. And hungry again you shall never be."

So the boy returned home, with no brothers but with the chicken feed. His father cried with joy when he saw his youngest son returned to him. Then they fed the king's chicken feed to the chickens.

And forever after, when those chickens laid eggs, the eggs were made of solid gold.

And the boy and his father lived happily ever after.

The creature stops speaking. He is still staring at you, but now with a satisfied expression on his strange, green face.

"That's it?" you ask.

He nods happily.

You gaze at the little creature. The magic you felt when he spoke is gone. He is a strange, lonely little swamp toad. Nothing more. Your voice is loud and angry when you say, "That had nothing to do with Yoda!" You rise to your feet—and hit your head, hard, on the ceiling. "Why are you wasting my time?"

The creature looks crestfallen. He turns away from you.

You sit back down and sigh. "I'll never be a Jedi at this rate."

The creature murmurs, "Why wish you become Jedi, hm?"

You stare at the flickering fire beneath the pot of root-leaf stew. "I don't know. To save the galaxy from the Empire. And to help my friends."

The creature peers at you, as if he knows there is more.

"And," you continue, "and . . . well . . . because of my father, I guess."

"Ah," says the creature, crawling up onto his little bed and sitting there. He kicks his short legs back and forth before him, like a small child. "Powerful Jedi was your father. Mmm."

You roll your eyes. "How do you know? You don't even know who I am! This is ridiculous!" You stand up—and hit your head on the ceiling again. You curse and turn toward the door. Just outside the window, R2 is jumping up and down, trying to get your attention.

"Beep beep beep boop boop!"

"Yeah, Artoo, we're leaving."

You're clambering over roots and chairs and stools to get to the door. Behind you, the creature closes his great green and black eyes. His voice is no more than a murmur. "I cannot teach him. He has no patience."

You hesitate at the door.

The creature is answered by a voice as vast and calm as the deserts of Tatooine: "He will learn patience."

You spin around. There is no one else in the room.

The creature says, "He is not ready. . . ."

"YODA!" you cry, staring at the strange little creature. "*You* are Yoda!"

Obi-Wan Kenobi's voice suffuses the little house: "Was I any better when you taught me?"

"He is too old," the creature—Yoda—replies. "Too old to begin the training."

You move swiftly to the side of his bed and kneel,

peering at the strange blue-green skin, wizened like a raisin, white wisps of hair flying in all directions from his otherwise bald scalp. He is hideous. He is ridiculous.

He is Yoda.

"Yoda, please," you say. "I've already learned so much. . . ." And then you pause, before saying, "I . . . I understand the story now. It *was* about Yoda."

The creature turns his luminous eyes upon you.

"*You* were the frog, the cat, the chicken, and the king. I was each of the three brothers."

"The *first* two brothers you were," Yoda says, pointing a gnarled finger in your face.

"I was," you say, and you let your head fall. "But I won't be. I will be the youngest boy. I will trust you. I will listen to you. I will learn." And then you add, "I'm not afraid."

Yoda's eyes darken. He rises up, taller and taller, until he seems to fill the room, until it seems that he is the greatest, grandest, largest creature you have ever met. "You will be," he intones, looking down at you, through you, and deep into you. "Oh, you will be."

LESSON MU:
THE FORCE IS NOT MULTIPLE CHOICE

So which are you, young Padawan? One of the older brothers? Or the youngest?

I know what you'd like to say. We'd all like to say that we're the youngest brother. But are you really?

Let's find out.

Are you familiar with those teen magazines that have multiple choice tests? You answer a bunch of questions, and if you chose mostly A, you're this kind of person, and mostly B, you're that other kind?

We're going to do one of those tests.

One question. Three options.

You might want to meditate before we begin.

Really.

Okay, have you meditated? Then here we go.

It's lunchtime in the school cafeteria. You exit the food line, gripping your tray of steaming sloppy joe. You look around.

To your right, you see your friends. The table is full, except for one chair next to your best friend. You know your best friend has been having a really rough day.

Straight ahead of you, there's a new kid. A group of mean kids has sat down around him. They look like they're already starting to give the kid a hard time.

To your left, there's someone in your class who sits alone every day. She would obviously like to sit with someone, but nobody gives her a chance.

So, do you:

A) Go sit beside your friend. He or she is your best friend, and needs your support today. The other kids can wait.

B) Sit down with the new student. If the mean kids tease him, you'll stand up to them, or at least let the new kid know you're on his side.

C) Join the table with the loner. She's been suffering the longest, and it's time to help her out.

Think about it. Which will it be?

All right, ready for the answer?

It's a trick question. Jedi do not act hypothetically. They act in real life. Next time you see A, B, or C going down, do something about it. For real.

That is the way of the Jedi.

CHAPTER FOURTEEN

YOU SIT, CROSS-LEGGED, before Yoda's little house. Your eyes are closed. You are listening. You are feeling.

Yoda is near you. You can faintly perceive the heat that emanates from him. Yoda is holding up an object. This is like an exercise you did with Ben once, back when he was your teacher. Back when he was alive.

"A stick?"

Yoda grunts angrily.

"A rock?"

"Guessing you are," he says. "Guess not. *Feel.*"

You try to still your mind. Quietly—oh, so quietly, you hear something moving. Small, quick movements. Not going-somewhere movements. More like . . .

squirming. There is heat coming from Yoda . . . but there is more heat, just a little more heat, coming from his hand.

"It's alive . . ." you murmur.

"Mmm . . ." Yoda says.

You get excited. "A frog!"

"No!" Yoda barks. You open your eyes. It's a mouse. "No," Yoda says again, shaking his froglike head. "Guess you do! Impatient you are! Trust the Force you do not." He looks away from you. "Eight hundred years have I trained Jedi. The deepest commitment must a Jedi have. The most serious mind." He grunts and puts down the mouse. It scurries away into the thick, wet greenery of Dagobah.

"You a long time have I watched," he says. "Always looking away you are—off to the horizon. Adventure! Excitement! Never your mind on *where you are*." Yoda punctuates those words by gesturing with his walking stick at your chest. "A Jedi looks not to other times, other places. To *now* a Jedi looks, and feels."

You nod. You are trying to understand. Trying, but not succeeding.

"Again your eyes you must close." You do. "What is around you? Every tree, rock, thing living and not living must you list."

You squint and try to remember your exact surroundings.

Suddenly, Yoda's stick *whacks* you in the side of the head. "Remember not!" Yoda commands, as if he is reading your thoughts. "*Feel.*"

You are sprinting through the jungle, leaping over stones and running along wet logs, trying to sense the slick spots, the rotten spots, before you step on them. Yoda is clinging to your neck. He is small, but his judgment of you, his disappointment, hangs heavier than his little body.

"*Focus*," he says.

You leap up onto a log that has fallen over a stream. As your foot lands on it, you relax. Inhale. You hear the hollow sound it makes, feel its weight beneath you, its density. You take two long strides and then—a short one. You hop over a pale spot and slide your feet the rest of the way, till you jump down onto the farther bank and keep running.

"Good," Yoda intones. "Felt the wood you did. Knew what was good, what rotten."

There is a steep slope that leads down into a wet ravine. A bunch of vines hang from a nearby tree. You go to grab one—and hesitate.

"*Feel*," Yoda whispers. You close your eyes and feel without touching. There is a strong vine among the bunch. A good, hearty one, ready and happy to bear your weight, and Yoda's. You open your eyes. It is obvious. It looks no different from the others. But it is different. You know it. You take it, swing out over the ravine, and drop lightly to the other side.

"Good! Good!"

You run, and run, and run. Your legs tire. But the Force is good, and as you relax into it, your legs keep moving as if this is what they were meant to do. Indeed, you think, it is. Your arms and shoulders ache from swinging and climbing and carrying Yoda. But you breathe deeply—then smile. This is what they were meant to do, too. It is their function. The soreness is just telling you that they are working to their potential. It is not bad pain. It is merely the language of your body, speaking. And you are, at last, listening.

You have stopped. Yoda stands, like a wizened, withered stump, staring into the distance. You sit cross-legged, feeling your breath come in through your nose, down your throat, into your chest, and out again.

"A Jedi's strength flows from the Force," Yoda is saying. "But beware of the dark side. Anger . . . fear . . . aggression . . . The dark side of the Force are they. Easily they flow, quick to join you in a fight. But if once you start down the dark path, forever will it dominate your destiny, consume you it will, as it did Obi-Wan's apprentice."

You lose track of your breathing. "Vader?" you ask. Yoda nods.

You have another question. "Yoda, is the dark side stronger?"

"No . . . no . . . Quicker, yes. Easier, yes. More seductive. Like a big cake of swamp cane. Eat it all, you want to, and sweet will it taste. Full will you feel. And energetic. But fade the energy will, and sick you soon will be. Better to eat fruit, fish, good things. Not as sweet. But long will they last."

You furrow your brow. "I know a cake when I see one. But what about the dark side? How do you tell the difference between the dark side and the Force?"

"Search your feelings, and know you will. Like the wood on the tree trunk. When you are calm. At peace. Not angry. Not grasping. You will know."

"But tell me why—"

Suddenly, Yoda is impatient. "No! No! There is no why. There only *is*, and *is not*. No more will I teach you today."

You don't know what you said that was so wrong. Disappointed, still hungry for knowledge, you stand. Stretch.

And then you see it.

Looming dark and sinister through the tangled branches of the jungle. It is a cave. Even from this distance—a hundred meters or more—you can feel it, like a sudden gust of freezing wind. "What . . . what is that place?" you ask. "I feel . . . cold . . . death . . ."

Yoda looks up at you, and his eyes are shining.

"That place . . . strong with the dark side it is. A domain of evil. In you must go."

"What . . . what's in there?" You can't take your eyes from its darkness, like a negative space, a void, among the vibrant, vivid greenery of the rest of the planet.

Yoda's voice is quiet, but clear. "Only what you take with you."

You pick up your lightsaber.

"Your weapons," Yoda says. "You will not need them."

You pause, look at Yoda. You look at the cave.

You keep the lightsaber in your hand.

The darkness is thick, and smells musty and rotten. But not rich, not full of life, breaking down and transforming into something new, like most of the rotting smells of Dagobah. This is a smell like death.

Something moves behind you. You turn. A black snake, long and thick, curls around a root that protrudes from the earthen walls. It is speckled with white spots—each one looks like a death's head. You shudder.

You push deeper into the cave. Creepers hang in your path. The air is cold here. A rush of wind blows something sticky into your face. You claw it off. It's a spider web—teeming with tiny arachnids. You try not to panic, flicking them from your skin, your ears, your hair.

Your heart is beating hard. Your breath is shallow.

You are afraid.

And angry. Angry at Yoda for sending you in here. For giving you all of these stupid tests and never being satisfied. For not recognizing how well you've done, how far you've come.

Also, you realize, you are angry at yourself. Angry that you are so afraid.

And then you hear something breathing in the darkness.

It sounds . . . metallic.

You step forward. Again. Once more.

And then he emerges from the shadows.

Darth Vader.

Darth Vader is here.

He has found you. Followed you here. Somehow.

You grab your lightsaber and ignite the blue blade.

His lightsaber rises, too—a pulsating red, reflecting in his black helm and black, synthetic eyes.

The blades are, in the darkness, strangely complementary. As if, somehow, they belong together.

Vader advances.

Fear and hatred mingle in your heart.

He raises his lightsaber. You raise yours sideways, and as his crashes down upon you, you catch it with your own, and your strength holds.

You step back. He advances, swinging his blade. You parry, sidestep. He turns to you, lightsaber coming round fast—but too late.

With a vicious strike, your lightsaber blade is already slicing through Darth Vader's neck.

His head rolls to the cave wall. His body crumples.

You stand astride it, heaving, victorious.

He is dead. Dead at last!

You turn your gaze on his head. His mask breaks asunder in a sudden explosion, revealing his life-less face—but it is not his face.

It is *your* face, staring back at you. Eyes wide. Mouth open.

Your face, in Vader's helmet.

You turn and run.

LESSON NU:
PATIENCE PLUS COMPASSION EQUALS STRENGTH

Think of someone you do not like. Someone you know who's been mean to you in the past, or whom you're afraid of, or whom, maybe, you're not always very nice to.

Think of everything you know about that person. Think of his parents, his family, his house, his schoolwork, his friends. Think of what he is good at, what he is bad at.

Now pretend you *are* him or her. Close your eyes and walk through the day in her shoes. You should imagine yourself with her joys, and with her pains. Can you name those pains? You should try. Really try.

Understand that person. As thoroughly as you can.

This will give you patience and compassion, the next time you encounter them. Which is good.

Patience and compassion, combined, make strength.

CHAPTER FIFTEEN

⬦

IN THE DARK HEART of the Empire's largest Star Destroyer, there is a dark room. In that dark room is a large, dark egg. It is a meditation chamber. In that large, dark egg is possibly the darkest soul in the galaxy.

"Lord Vader," Admiral Piett murmurs. He has hurried from the bridge, from where the destroyer is navigating a particularly nasty asteroid field. His hands are shaking. For lots of reasons.

Slowly, the dark egg cracks open. Vader is sitting with his back to the admiral. His helmet is off. Piett averts his eyes. Even the back of Vader's head is difficult to look at—flour-white skin, scars and burns crisscrossing the surface.

The helmet is lowered. The skin is sheathed in the shining alloy of Vader's black helm. He turns. "What is it?"

Vader's voice inspires uncontrollable shivers of fear, no matter how many times one hears it. The admiral, though, has a message even more terrifying. He swallows hard before saying, "The Emperor commands you to make contact with him."

Vader's reaction is swift. "Move the ship out of the asteroid field so that we have clear transmission."

"Yes, my lord." The admiral scurries away. Vader steps from his meditation cell and strides to a small platform—the transmitter deck. He steps onto it. He kneels. He bows his head.

The sight of Vader bowing should strike fear in any heart. For it means there is one more powerful, more evil, than he. And that one is come.

A projection fills the room, from floor to ceiling. It depicts a figure in a black cloak, hooded like a Jedi's. Under the hood, barely visible, is a hideous face. Wrinkles deep and regular as a castle's moat run in concentric lines from temple to chin and under the sunken eyes. Those eyes are a rich yellow, with piercing black pupils. Vader sees none of this. His head is still bowed.

"What is thy bidding, Master?"

The Emperor's voice is deep, like Vader's. But it is raspy, too. More of a croak than a voice. "There is a great disturbance in the Force."

Vader nods, not raising his head. "I have felt it."

The Emperor inhales—as if drawing breath through a reed in a swamp. "We have a new enemy. Luke Skywalker."

Vader's head does not move, but a new tension grips his hunched shoulders, his bent neck. "Yes, my master."

"He could destroy us," the Emperor croaks.

For a moment, Vader does not speak. When he does, his rich voice is slow and deliberate. "He is just a boy. Obi-Wan can no longer help him."

"The Force is strong with him," the Emperor says. "The son of Skywalker must *not* become a Jedi."

Vader raises his head to his master—a new idea occurring to him, it seems. "If he could be turned, he would become a powerful ally."

Pause. The Emperor's gaze considers his most promising pupil, penetrating that dark helm, that black mask, through his apprentice's burnt and scarred skin, and down into his dark heart. There, in the center of evil, the Emperor detects . . . something. . . . He cannot tell what it is.

"Yes," he croaks at last. "Yes, he would be a great asset." And then, "Can it be done?"

Darth Vader bows his head again.

"He will join us or die, my master."

CHAPTER SIXTEEN

---◆---

YOU ARE STANDING on your hands. Yoda is balancing on your feet. The blood has rushed to your face. Rivers of sweat are running down your arms and your neck, and taste salty in your mouth. The air is thick and wet around you.

"Relax you must," Yoda murmurs. "Use the Force. Think you must not. Strain you must not. Breathe. Rooted you must be. Like a tree."

There are two stones before you, each about the size of a grapefruit.

"Now," Yoda murmurs, "the stone. Feel it."

You focus on the smaller of the two stones. Slowly, it begins to rise. Untouched by anything but your thoughts, and the Force. You lift it, move it, until it rests on top of the other stone.

You have returned to the fen where the X-wing crashed. It has been sinking deeper and deeper into the muck each day. Your supplies are still stacked in messy piles on the bank. As you hold yourself upside down, and focus on keeping one stone balanced on the other, R2-D2 starts beeping frantically.

"Focus . . ." Yoda purrs.

Still concentrating on the stones, you glance over at R2-D2. He's standing by the X-wing.

The ship is sliding rapidly into the swamp. At this rate, it will be gone within minutes.

"Concentrate!" Yoda cries. Too late. You go toppling over, throwing the little Jedi to the ground. The stones fall.

You jump to your feet and run to the edge of the swamp. You stare. Only a tip of a wing of the fighter is still visible. R2 continues beeping frantically.

"We'll never get it out now!"

Yoda appears beside you, dusting himself off from his fall. "So certain are you. Always with you it cannot be done. Hear you nothing I say? Understand you nothing?"

You shake your head, staring at your only means of getting off this fetid, stinking swamp-planet—as it disappears into the muck.

Yoda gestures at the ship. You know what that gesture means.

You look between him and the X-wing. You shake your head. "Master! Moving stones is one thing. This is totally different."

"No! Not different. Difference is in your mind only. You must unlearn what you have learned."

You shake your head. "Okay. I'll try."

"No. Try not. Do. Or do not. There is no try."

You take a deep breath. Focus on the ship. You reach out your hand and grip the ship with your mind. It is enormous.

You wrap your mind around every corner, press your thoughts into every edge.

Your mind probes the swamp around the ship.

You begin to lift.

It rises.

And rises.

You feel its weight. Its enormity. It is ten of you. Twenty. Fifty. You strain against it. *Don't disappoint Yoda*, you think.

Your concentration is beginning to waver. You are straining. The ship starts to sink.

Don't disappoint him.

It sinks entirely.

"I can't," you say, bowing your head. You are exhausted. "It's too big."

Yoda peers up at you. "Size matters not. Look at me. Judge me by my size, do you?"

You shake your head.

"Be not the older sons. Judge me not as a toad. Nor a cat. Nor a king. Nor a man. I am both. I am all." Suddenly, Yoda pinches you.

"Ow!"

"This flesh deceives you. Yes, today you look like a man, and the ship looks like a ship. But you are not, and it is not. Shapes of the Force you are. One and the same. Reach out with your feelings you must; part of all things you are. Particles we are, waves, all one." He holds you in his gaze. "A candle's light you see. The candle I hide with my hand. The candle I reveal. Different light? No. One light. Separated by my hand." He turns to the swamp. "So with you and the ship. One you are. Just separated."

Your shoulders go limp. You are so confused, so tired. "I don't know," you say. "I think you're describing the impossible."

Yoda shakes his head. He closes his eyes and reaches out a small, withered hand. Birds are singing in the ancient trees. The forest is thick and still. Calmly, with a face relaxed and at peace, little Yoda raises his hand.

The X-wing begins to rise, rise, rise, up out of the swamp. Ten metric tons of steel and circuits hover over the surface of the water, and then travel, slowly, steadily, to the shore. Yoda, all thirteen kilograms of him, lowers his hand, and the fighter

comes to rest on the mossy, root-strewn bank.

"I . . ." you stammer. "I don't believe it . . ."

Yoda nods.

"That is why you fail."

LESSON XI:
DO NOT STAND ON YOUR HANDS AND LIFT ROCKS

Don't worry, young one. I don't except you to stand on your hands and move stones around, or to lift a spaceship with your mind.

I mean, that'd be cool. If you can do it, go for it.

But I don't expect you to.

Instead, try this: first, meditate for ten seconds.

Then, stand on one foot. Or put a book on your head.

Count to ten.

Okay? Now, while still balancing, say your telephone number, *backward*.

Can you do that? If so, keep balancing, but now, spell your first name backward.

Now, if you're somewhere you can, stand on one foot *and* balance a book on your head, and then spell your *full* name backward.

Try not to get frustrated. Breathe. Use instant meditation to stay calm.

If this is hard, that's okay. Just keep doing it. Not *trying* to do it, mind you. Just do it again and again and again until it isn't so hard. Until you can balance on one foot and keep a book on your head and spell your full name backward—with a smile.

And then you might be ready to move rocks and space-ships with your mind.

Maybe.

CHAPTER SEVENTEEN

YOUR EYES ARE CLOSED. The breath whistles in and out of you, like water running through a thin pipe. The corners of your mouth edge up. It is pleasant to be at peace.

The sounds and smells of Dagobah are exploding. A bird with a raspy, echoing caw announces that the tree twenty paces forward and forty paces to your left is *his* tree. And don't you forget it. You can't see the bird, or the tree, of course, because your eyes are closed. But you can hear him, and sense him, and you try to tell him, *Fine. It's your tree. Enjoy.*

It rained last night, and the smell of the ground is rich with all the plants and worms and millipedes that love it when the earth is soggy. They are churning the loam over and over in their little underground farms. You can sense each one.

"Good," Yoda says. "Good. Feel. Sense. Smell. Hear. Mm. Your eyes closed you must keep. Test you now, I will. Calm you must stay. Still you must be. Holding something, I am. Sense it, and tell me."

You breathe out through your nose, pouring out your silvery, fluid breath. You draw it in again.

His hand is outstretched. Something sits on his hand. You can hear its rapid heartbeat. So it is alive. And small. Last time it was a mouse, so maybe this time—no, don't think it through. Just sense it. The creature is lying flat, its belly—

"Luke!" Yoda rasps.

You smile. He's trying to distract you.

"Open your eyes you must!"

You shake your head and retrain your focus on Yoda's outstretched hand. Where is his outstretched hand? Has he moved it? Your smile fades. You are concentrating.

"Luke!"

You are jerked back and forth. Yoda has grabbed your shirt. He is shaking you.

You laugh quietly. "Oh, no, Master. You told me to keep my eyes closed. Nice try, though. You're holding a small animal in your hand. I'm going to sense what it is."

"Sense what is coming out of the jungle you should!"

Your smile disappears again. But still your eyes are closed. You throw your attention to the woods. A distant boom, accompanied by the sounds of branches snapping and brush being crushed. Again. And again.

"It's a . . ." you say. "It's a . . ."

"Keep your eyes closed if you like!" Yoda croaks. "Running I am!"

Your eyelids pop open.

Your mouth falls agape.

Coming through the trees, directly for you, is an enormous elephoth.

Its hide is green and thick as armor. Its two

thick tusks jut straight out from its mouth, like the blasters on a snow walker. They are greenish, and covered with moss and vines, like fallen trees. It has two trunks protruding from its face, and they writhe like angry snakes.

The elephoth stands as tall as a small tree, and weighs probably as much as your X-wing. Its legs are thick and round as hornbeam trunks. Its small red eyes gaze around madly.

You look over your shoulder. Yoda is hopping over fallen tree trunks and waddling away from you as fast as he can. He is making pretty good time.

You look back at the elephoth.

And then you remember R2. He's doing some maintenance on his memory core. You spin around. Lights are flashing on his body, but his audio and visual processors must be temporarily offline, because he hasn't started screaming and cursing at you yet. If he had seen the elephoth, he would have invented *new* curse words by now.

You spin back toward the rampaging beast. It

tramples the earth and is twice as close to you as it was before. Could you outrun it? Maybe. But not if you had to carry R2 with you.

So you reach for your lightsaber. You ignite it.

The blue light catches the elephoth's small red eyes. It rears back, like a tree uprooting itself, and blasts a double cry, one from each trunk, in wrenching harmony. The jungle echoes.

You breathe. You straighten your spine. You smile. You hear. You feel. You sense. You raise your pulsating blade.

And then you hear another blast, also in the distinctive harmony of elephoth trunks. But this one is shriller, and far away.

The cry enrages the elephoth before you. It rears up again, and then comes crashing down.

"Beeeeeeeeeep! Beeeeeep beep beep beep beep boop!"

R2 has woken up. Great.

"Beep beep boooooooop!"

You try to focus on the elephoth again, and not

the unrepeatable things R2 is emitting from his speakers.

The elephoth is coming for you. You grip your lightsaber. It is ten meters away.

Eight.

Six.

Four.

Almost close enough for your blade.

Two meters away.

You bolt to the right, waving your lightsaber above your head.

The enraged elephoth follows.

You bound over a fallen tree trunk, plant your foot on a flat stone, leap across a mucky patch of thick moss, and begin to run. Still, you wave your lightsaber above your head.

You don't have to look back. You can feel the elephoth following you. And hear it. It's pretty loud.

Ahead there is a tangle of brambles. You slash it with your blade and run directly through it. The elephoth roars its two tones. Somewhere ahead of you, the roar is answered. The crash of the great beast's footsteps are falling ever so slightly behind.

Four meters.

Six meters.

Eight.

You slow your pace.

Eight meters.

Six.

Okay. That's close enough.

A ravine is ahead of you. You can see it, thick with ferns and vines and half-rotted trees still standing somehow.

You dance across a fallen log, sensing the good wood without having to hesitate even for a moment. As soon as you jump off it, the elephoth steps on it, sending it splintering into the air. You jerk your head to the left as a chunk of sharp wood hurtles past your ear. From behind. You felt it before it happened. You try not to smile.

You arrive at the edge of the ravine. Vines hang like a quiver of arrows. One of them is good and strong and ready to bear your weight. You ignore it. You turn off your lightsaber, sheath it, and then slide down the side of the ravine.

The elephoth slows. It doesn't like steep slopes. You had not reckoned on that.

You break your fall with your feet, slowing the slide down the slope. You reach for your lightsaber.

You ignite your blade and wave it above your head. The response is the frantic two-tone call of an elephoth, coming from the bottom of the ravine. Above you, the call is answered.

And then there is thunder. The great beast with the tree-trunk tusks is charging down the slope behind you.

Twelve meters.

Six.

Two.

You plant your feet and hurl yourself away from the ravine wall, hurtling across the space of the ravine, arms flailing, legs kicking, hair flying, before you crash into the opposite wall, a good ten meters away. You did not know you could jump ten meters. As it turns out, you can.

Your cheek hits the twiggy, root-woven earth. It explodes around you. You grip the soil and turn around.

The elephoth has stumbled to the bottom of the ravine. Its great tusks are covered with half the forest that you ran through to escape it. But it has calmed. For beside it is a much smaller elephoth. That smaller elephoth is rubbing its great domed head against his mother's flank. And she is exploring his face with her two huge trunks.

You smile, pull yourself to your feet, and climb up the side of the ravine.

At the top of the slope, Yoda is sitting on a stump. He is watching the two elephoths.

You look at him expectantly.

He says, "Next time I tell you to open your eyes, listen you might." Then he crawls down from the stump and hobbles off toward home.

He is laughing quietly.

LESSON OMICRON:
KEEPING TRACK OF EVERYTHING ISN'T EASY

You're going to need an assistant for this one.

I want you to stand on one foot, or to balance a book on your head. Breathe. Meditate for ten seconds.

Now, while you're balancing, your assistant is going to read the following riddle to you. You should NOT read the riddle before this begins. The whole point is for you to focus, relax, and think clearly—all while standing on one foot or balancing a book on your head.

Okay. Get in position. Meditate.

Hello, assistant. This is the riddle. Read it aloud:

A city bus is on its route. At its first stop, it picks up ten passengers.

At its second stop, the big white bus whines to a stop, opens its doors, lets off two passengers, and picks up four more.

At the third stop, its brakes screech, it lets off two more passengers, and picks up six.

At its fourth stop, it hisses as it comes to rest. The doors jerk open. No one gets off, and four people get on.

At its fifth stop, with the sun glinting off its windshield, five people get on and six people get off.

Okay? Got all that?

What color was the bus?

Don't know? You should keep balancing. Your assistant should read the riddle again.

Did it?

Okay, this time the question is: How many people got off the bus at the fourth stop?

Don't know? Last chance. Read it one more time.

Now: How many people are on the bus after the fifth stop?

I know, this test seems cruel. So many things to keep track of! But when you're being chased by a raging elephoth—or worse, fighting a Sith Lord—you've got to keep track of many things at once. And stay peaceful, sensitive, and patient through it all.

I warned you. Being a Jedi ain't easy.

CHAPTER EIGHTEEN

———————————— ⟨⟩ ————————————

"**GOOD, GOOD**," Yoda whispers. "The Force you should feel, flowing in you and out of you, like breath. Calm. Yes. Through the Force, things you will see. Other places. The future . . . the past . . . old friends long gone . . ."

Your legs are crossed, your eyes closed. You are outside his small house. The air is hot and wet. You are breathing. Listening to Yoda and breathing.

"But beware these visions you must. Control the future you cannot. It shifts. We can try to change it, but we are small, and sometimes we push one way, and the future, another way it goes."

The jungle feels silent. It doesn't *sound* silent. It *feels* silent.

"Never understood this did Vader."

Your eyes fly open.

"Calm . . ." says Yoda. "Breathe you must, and listen."

You close your eyes again.

"Vader saw the future, but try to control it he did. Anger he felt, and fear. Led him to the dark side. Quick way. Easy way. But not good way."

Yoda chuckles. You don't know why. You open your eyes and glance at his gnarled, withered body. His smile is as serene as the double sunset of Tatooine.

"Story heard I once," he says. "From my master. True or not, I do not know. But good story. Listen you will."

Yoda closes his eyes, inhales slowly, and begins.

"There was once a Jedi named K'ungfu.

"Wise was K'ungfu, and strong. But at this time, none was wiser or stronger than the great Jedi Master Chuang.

"One day, heard did K'ungfu that Master Chuang's apprentice had died.

"So Master K'ungfu sent a messenger to Chuang, his condolences to give.

"But when arrived the messenger did, found he the Great Jedi—laughing! With his friends, he was. Playing music, singing, joking. There, the body of Chuang's apprentice lay, and laugh Chuang did!

"Upset the messenger was. 'Is this,' he asked, 'how behaves a great Jedi when his apprentice dies?'

"To the messenger the Great Jedi replied, 'Beat my head should I? Tear my clothes should I? Weep and wail in the streets should I? Moved, the Force has. It was in the form of my apprentice. Now, different my apprentice looks. Still. Quiet. Soon, part of the ground will he be. Should I be angry? Is my apprentice less pleased, being a different part of the Force? Being trees growing, or the sea dancing and roaring in the wind? If he is pleased, why should I cry? And if I should change,' the Great Jedi went on, 'if my back should hunch, if my hair should fall out, if my skin should sag like a sack—or worse, if my elbow turns into a rooster, and my knee a cat—cry should I then? No. I shall wonder at the miraculous changes the Force has wrought. Choose, I do not, what happens to me, or to my apprentice. So cry I do not. Better to sing, it is.'

"Returned, did the messenger, to Master K'ungfu. When related had the messenger what the Great Jedi had said, K'ungfu closed his eyes. 'Of course,' he said, smiling and nodding. 'Much to learn have I.'"

Yoda stops speaking.

In that moment, something comes into your head. A vision. An awful vision. Your eyes fly open. Yoda is staring at you curiously.

"Han!" you cry. "Leia!"

Yoda's face falls.

"I see them!" And you do. They are in pain. They are being tortured. Leia is screaming, her eyes bulging from her head. Han is straining, his back arched, his neck on the verge of snapping.

"The future you see," Yoda murmurs. "A future."

"I've got to help them!" you cry.

Yoda shakes his head. "Hear me you do not."

"I've got to go to them! I've got to save them!"

Yoda pauses. "Decide you must how to serve them best. If you leave now, help them you could. But likely you would destroy all that they have worked for, all for which they have fought and suffered. The cause. The Rebellion. Their battle against the Emperor. All would be lost. But saved could they be."

You stare at the tiny Jedi Master. Your eyes are wild.

The silence dies in the jungle, replaced by a riot of sound.

LESSON PI:
TOUGH CHOICES

When I gave you the multiple choice test a few lessons ago, I said that Jedi don't act hypothetically. I told you that you couldn't choose between sitting with your friend, or helping the new kid, or sitting with the lonely girl. You had to do them all.

Which was true.

But there are times, rare times, when you cannot do everything. When you have to choose between two bad options. Bad options like:

1) letting your friends suffer and perhaps die; and

2) saving them, but not being skilled enough to face Vader and not strong enough to resist the dark side. Which would result in dooming the galaxy to slavery for the next few hundred years. That's a tough choice.

But there are more mundane examples of the same conundrum. For example, you are going on vacation with your best friend. You're going somewhere awesome, like an amusement park or the mountains. It is going to be the best trip of your life, and of your best friend's life.

But you are also trying to change schools, to go somewhere with better academics and more interesting teachers. And the entrance exam has just been scheduled for *during* your trip.

What do you do?

Do you let your friend down, and take the exam?

Or do you give up on your dream of this new school, and go on vacation with your pal?

There is no right answer.

But the choices you make will shape you.

And they may shape history, too.

CHAPTER NINETEEN

I T IS NIGHT. The X-wing's lights glow faintly against the gloom of the swamp. R2-D2 checks the readings on various panels. He is whirring like a silverfinch. He has no love for Dagobah. You are loading your belongings into the cargo hold.

Yoda's wrinkled face looks pained. "Luke, please! Complete the training you must!"

You shake your head. The vision refuses to leave you.

Your best friends—in terrible pain. Weeping. Screaming.

"You must not go!" Yoda insists. The deep shadows of night envelop his small form.

"They'll die if I don't."

Suddenly, another voice answers you. Rich and kind and understanding.

Ben's voice. "You don't know that, Luke."

You turn, and see him. He is standing beside Yoda. He shimmers.

"Ben!" you cry. "Are you . . . Aren't you . . . ?"

Obi-Wan Kenobi smiles. "I am still a part of the Force. You have, through your training, learned to see me."

You stare, drinking in the sight of your first master, your friend.

"Please, Luke," he says. "Please listen to Yoda."

Your shoulders hunch. He doesn't understand. He's just like Yoda. "I can help them! I can feel the Force!"

"But you cannot control it. More importantly, you cannot control your feelings." Ben's eyes are anxious—you can see that, even through their otherworldly shimmer. He goes on. "This is a dangerous time for you. You will be tempted by the dark side."

"Yes!" Yoda agrees. "Listen to Obi-Wan! Remember your failure at the cave!"

"But I've learned so much since then."

Ben's voice is rasping and low. "Luke, it is *you* the Emperor wants. That's why he makes your friends suffer."

You stop. You think about that. The Emperor wants *you*? A strange mixture of fear and—and something else—is shifting, taking shape, in your heart.

Yoda and Obi-Wan watch you.

"Luke," Ben says. "I don't want to lose you the way I lost Vader."

You look into his old, sad eyes. You feel that *something* in your heart start to fade. To be replaced by love for the old man who trained you and gave his life for you. You look to Yoda. Yoda, for whom there is no distinction between a mouse and you and a spaceship. Who has devoted his life to training Jedi so that they may help others. Yoda, who had so much patience, when you had none.

"You won't lose me," you say to them. "I promise."

"Stopped they must be," Yoda says. "On this all depends. If you choose the quick and easy path, as Vader did, you will fall under his control, and an agent of evil you will become."

"If you choose to face Vader," Ben says, "you must do it alone. I cannot help you."

You nod. "I understand. Artoo, fire up the converters."

The little droid whistles happily.

"Luke!" Ben says desperately. "Don't give in to pride, fear, hatred. They lead to the dark side!"

You climb onto the wing of your fighter, and then put a leg into the cockpit.

"Strong is Vader," Yoda intones. "Mind what you have learned. Help you it can."

"I will." You slide into the pilot's seat. "And I'll return to finish my training. I promise." But already you're thinking of something else. Of Han and Leia. Of the Emperor. Of Vader.

You flip a switch. The cockpit hatch begins to close.

Outside the ship, Yoda says quietly to Ben, "Told you I did. Now, matters are worse."

"That boy is our last hope," Ben replies.

As your ship lifts into the sky, Yoda follows it with his gaze. "No . . ." he says at last. "There is another."

STRANGE
PLANETS

— PART II —

CHAPTER TWENTY

THE *MILLENNIUM FALCON* screams out of the atmosphere of Hoth, heading straight for a Star Destroyer.

This is less like a mouse running at a tiger, and more like a lame rabbit with one bad eye running at a tiger.

Leia, crouched over Han Solo's shoulder, mutters, "Uh, Han . . . ?"

He ignores her. "Chewie, prepare to make the jump to lightspeed."

C-3PO, who has been trying to get Han's attention since the hangar in the rebel base, tries again. "But, sir!"

Two laser blasts erupt from the destroyer and whizz past the *Falcon*'s hull. Four small Imperial fighters—TIEs—detach from a nearby formation and head directly for Solo's ship.

The tiger has buddies. Hardly seems fair.

"They're coming . . ." Leia murmurs.

Han just grins. "Yeah? Watch this."

He throws the lightspeed thruster down and turns to watch the stars go blazing by as the ship jumps into hyperspace.

But the stars do not go blazing by. They hang there, limp and static.

"Watch what?"

Han throws the thruster again. Nothing.

Very quietly, he says, "I think we're in trouble."

"If I may say so," C-3PO cuts in, "I noticed earlier that the hyperdrive motivator has been damaged. It's impossible to go to lightspeed!"

"We're in trouble!" Han shouts.

Explosions rock the ship as the four TIE fighters close in. Han grabs the steering column, turns the *Falcon* sharply, and guns it.

But the TIE fighters are hard on their backs.

Behind the fighters, the Imperial Star Destroyer lumbers after them all, cannons blazing.

Han jumps from the captain's seat. "Take it!" he shouts at Leia.

"What?"

He ignores her and runs to the mechanical port, where Chewbacca is already yanking at wires and crying in confusion. (Which sounds like "Arrrrraaaaragh!")

Leia watches the steering column veer left.

"Hey!" Han calls.

So the princess slides into the seat. She pushes hard left, exaggerating the turn.

"HEY!" Han cries, as he crashes into Chewbacca, and a cascade of sparks rain down on his scruffy head.

The TIE fighters bank and follow Leia's course, their lasers exploding all around the pirate ship.

Leia dips.

Han's head hits the ceiling. "Hey!"

The fighters follow.

Leia pulls up.

Han is thrown to the ground. "Hey!"

Leia smiles.

The *Falcon* rises, and rises, and rises—and then jolts violently.

"Arrrarraaraaragh!"

"That wasn't a laser!" Han barks. "We *hit* something!"

He mutters about "women pilots" and sprints back to the cockpit. "What are you *doing* princ—" He stops mid sentence. He sees what she sees.

"Asteroid field!" Leia announces grimly.

Indeed, stretching out before them as far as anyone can see are a million space rocks—some large, some small, some the size of tiny moons. A good two-thirds of them are large enough to destroy a spaceship like the *Falcon* on impact.

"Oh, boy," Han mutters. He slides into the pilot's seat, relieving Leia of her duties—which she performed more than admirably, it should be said, for the TIE fighters are now some distance behind—and stares at the death trap that stretches out before them.

The rocks hang there, deadly and silent.

The TIE fighters are closing in.

Han pushes forward on the steering column.

"Wait!" Leia says. "You're not going *into* the asteroid field?"

Han grins. "They'd be crazy to follow us."

Chewie, appearing in the doorway of the cockpit, sees his captain's course and howls.

Leia puts her head near Han's and whispers furiously: "You don't have to do this to impress me!"

"Sir!" C-3PO chirrups frantically. "The odds of successfully navigating an asteroid field are approximately 3,720 to 1!"

As if to demonstrate the droid's point, the first of the pursuing TIE fighters meets an asteroid head-on. It explodes.

Han grits his teeth. "Never tell me the odds. . . ."

———

Asteroids twirl and dance around them like some chaotic cosmic ballet. Someone who appreciates the beauty of the Force might enjoy watching the passing, spinning, whirling space boulders that hurtle past the *Falcon*. Han, Leia, Chewie, and C-3PO, on the other hand, are trying not to soil their pants. Except that Chewie and C-3PO don't wear pants.

Behind them, a second fighter collides with an asteroid, becoming a fiery, ephemeral grave.

"Well, Princess," Han sighs, "you said you wanted to be around when I made a mistake. This could be it."

"I take it back!" cries Leia. A small asteroid bounces off their hull with a sickening crunch. "I take it back!"

Beneath them, one of the enormous asteroids floats by, silent and inexorable as death. Han looks down at it. "I'm going to take us closer to one of the big ones."

"Closer?!" Leia and C-3PO and Chewie all cry

at once, though Chewie's "Closer?!" actually sounds like "Aaarararaagh?!"

The *Millennium Falcon* dives, and the TIE fighters follow. Soon, they are zipping over the craterous surface of the moon-sized asteroid, the TIE fighters in pursuit. The *Falcon* roars over a star-blue cliff edge and then dives into a canyon. The fighters follow, close behind, firing off an occasional potshot as they try to follow Han's reckless course.

"Oh, this is suicide!" C-3PO screams.

And then, it's over.

The canyon, that is. Nothing but a blue stone wall. "Hold on!" Han shouts, far too late. The *Falcon* rises straight up. The passengers go flying. The ship's belly is scraping the asteroid's blue stone. Han is wrestling with the controls, trying to pull up higher, higher, into the black sky above.

Below them, the two TIE fighters slam into the wall and explode.

C-3PO and Leia pull themselves to their feet, and then grip the walls again. The *Falcon* is now doing a slow flip. They both slide up the walls until they are plastered against the ceiling, and then slide down to the floor again.

Leia, on her knees, says, "I love it when you drive."

"There," Han says. "That looks pretty good."

"*What* looks good?"

C-3PO, sitting on the floor, says, "I have not registered a single good thing about this situation, sir. Of all the situations I have been in, which number some eight million, three hundred thou—"

"Aaarararagh," says Chewbacca. Which means, roughly translated, "Shut up."

The *Falcon* is heading back toward the asteroid now. On the surface there is a small black cave.

Han is heading straight for it.

Leia says, "No."

Han says, "Yup."

"I hope you know what you're doing," she mutters.

"Yeah," Han replies. "Me, too."

A moment later, the *Millennium Falcon* disappears into the cave on the face of the asteroid.

LESSON RHO:
NAVIGATING AN ASTEROID FIELD

This next test needs to be done in a room that belongs to you, because you need to get that room messy. Put objects all over the floor. Toys, books, pillows, whatever. If you're outside, maybe you can use stones, twigs, and book bags.

Now, stand on one leg. Breathe. Feel your breath pass from your nose, down your throat, into your stomach, down your rooted leg, and into the ground.

When you feel fully rooted, start hopping. Hop from one end of the room to the other, without touching anything, including the strewn objects.

Whether you're in an asteroid field or the jungle on Dagobah, as a Jedi you must feel what is around you, must take it into your mind, and respond to it as if it were a part of your very body. According to Yoda, after all, it is.

If this test is easy, try it with your eyes closed.

CHAPTER TWENTY-ONE

N THE ASTEROID, it is as dark as the insides of a tauntaun. It doesn't smell quite as bad, though.

A tunnel, just large enough for the *Falcon*, winds into the core of the blue space stone.

Han follows it. Slowly.

"What are we doing here?" Leia whispers.

"Ararrraaaragh," Chewie says. Which means the same thing.

"We need a safe place for repairs. Can't face those Star Destroyers again with no hyperdrive motivator."

The ship wends deeper and deeper into the asteroid. It is like entering a new world. A new world where there is no light, no sound—no sensations at all.

C-3PO informs the crew that "there are no official records of exploration of the center of asteroids. That means it might be quite dangerous."

Everyone finds his commentary extremely insightful.

Han brings the ship to a bumpy landing in the blackness of the cave. "Hey, Chewie," he says, climbing out of the pilot's seat, "come help."

The pirate starship sits for hours in darkness, as Han and Chewbacca touch wires together and screw and unscrew bolts they don't really recognize. C-3PO tries to supervise them, regularly giving unhelpful advice. Leia stays in the cockpit, watching the readings on the dials.

After a while, Han joins her there. C-3PO follows him, nattering away. "I wonder, sir, if attaching the cobalt wire to crimson wire was really such a good idea. Not that I'm questioning your authority, sir. Your expertise, perhaps. But never your authority."

"Okay," says Han, ignoring the droid and addressing Leia. "I'm going to shut down the main—"

Suddenly, the ship lurches violently to the right. The three inhabitants of the cockpit are thrown against blinking control panels. The *Falcon* settles. They stand, not moving, barely breathing.

"Sir," C-3PO reports, "it is quite possible that this asteroid is not entirely stable."

"Not *entirely* stable?" Han replies. "I'm glad you're here to tell us these things. Not *entirely* stable. Professor, why don't you go help Chewie with the hyperdrive? See if he appreciates your analysis."

C-3PO totters out of the cockpit, muttering to himself about understanding over six million languages, but not quite having mastered the one called *sarcasm*.

The ship lurches again—even more violently this time. Han is thrown into the control panel again, while Leia is thrown into Han's arms.

The ship settles. He smiles at her.

"Let go!" she snaps.

"Don't get excited, Princess," he replies. He does not let go.

She pushes him away. "Being held by you, Captain, isn't quite enough to get me excited."

What follows is a flirtation that kind of looks like a fight—or maybe it's a fight that kind of looks like flirtation. I've never been very good at telling the difference. Anyway, it's irrelevant to your training, so I'm skipping it. Suffice it to say that Han and Leia end up kissing. If that sort of thing interests you, you can imagine it yourself.

And then C-3PO interrupts the kiss, announcing that Chewbacca has made a breakthrough with the hyperdrive motivator. Han comes very close to disabling the golden droid and affixing him to the exterior of the *Falcon* as a hood ornament. But he follows the droid to the mechanical bay to see what Chewie's done.

Not five minutes later, Leia shouts from the cockpit. Han and Chewbacca come running. The princess is pointing into the darkness. Her face is as white as her royal tunic. "There's something . . . something out there . . ."

Just as she says it, an object lands somewhere on the *Falcon*. Han listens.

A sound rises out of the darkness.

Regular. Persistent. Almost like something is gnawing on the ship. A panel of lights in the cockpit flickers and winks out.

"I'm going out there," Han says.

"Are you serious?"

"We just got this bucket of bolts back together. I'm not going to let something tear it apart."

"Or eat it. . . ." Leia mutters.

Han ducks from the cockpit. "Wait!" Leia shouts. "I'm coming with you!"

"Aaararararagh!" says Chewbacca, which means, "Me, too!"

The scruffy space pirate, the princess, and the walking mop don oxygen masks to enable breathing in the nearly nonexistent atmosphere of the asteroid. Han lowers the gangway, and he, Leia, and Chewbacca slowly make their way down it. Han is carrying a blaster. Chewbacca has his bowcaster, which is like a crossbow that uses magnets to fire energy bolts. (You should definitely ask for one of those for your next birthday. I know I'm going to.)

As the small group steps from the steel gangway to the floor of the asteroid, Leia says, "It's damp out here. And warmer than I expected."

Han tries to gaze through the darkness, but he can't make out much. Somewhere in the distance is the sound of dripping water.

"I have a bad feeling about this place," whispers the princess.

"I can't imagine why," Han replies.

Chewbacca barks and points to the ship's cockpit. A two-meter-long shape can be seen gliding across

the top of
the *Falcon*,
like a barracuda
swimming through
the dark waters of an
ocean reef.

Han turns on a heel and lets loose a laser
blast. The creature screeches, beating leath-
ery wings against the dark. Han shoots
again. It falls to the cave floor.
Han, followed by the oth-
ers, hurries to its crumpled
form. He kicks it with his
boot, moving a large wing
away from its huge, gnarled, batlike face. Leia shudders. So does Chewie.

"What I thought," says Han. "Mynocks. Probably chewing on the power cables. Chewie, check
the rest of the ship. Last thing we need in a fight
with a Star Destroyer is—"

"Watch out!" Leia shouts. Swooping out of the darkness is a pack of them, their toothy mouths screeching, their flattened noses hissing, their horrible eyes wide.

"Run!" Han cries, firing into the swarm of cold-blooded, leather-winged parasites.

Chewie and Leia sprint for the *Falcon*'s gangway.

Han fires again, his shot going low and hitting the floor of the cave.

Suddenly, the asteroid is sliding again, listing to the right. As the small crew of the *Falcon* tries to regain their footing, the mynocks descend upon them, swarming, their claws and sucking mouths lunging at hair, clothes, skin.

Han looks desperately around. With one arm, he covers his head. With the other, he levels his blaster at the ground by his feet—which is hard, he has suddenly realized, but not *rock* hard. He fires. The asteroid lurches again.

"Time to go!" he cries. They all manage to crawl

or stumble up the gangway, frantically swatting the mynocks away with arms and elbows, blasters and a crossbow. Chewbacca turns and pulverizes one last mynock as the hatch begins to close.

Once the hatch is secure, Han leads a mad dash for the cockpit. "We're getting out of here!"

"The star cruisers will be waiting for us!" Leia objects, running after him. "Is it really—"

"No time to discuss this in committee!" Han snaps. "Chewie, initiate the engines!"

Leia growls at him, "I am *not* a committee!"

As they come tumbling into the cockpit, C-3PO says, "Sir, I really think it's time for us to consider leaving."

"You know, goldenrod, I think this is the first time we've seen eye to eye. I'm so glad!"

"Oh! So am I, sir! So am I!"

Han rolls his eyes, initiates the lifters, and the ship lurches off the rock floor of the cave. Han pushes on the accelerator, and the *Falcon* leans forward, picking up speed. He steers them through the winding tunnel, his fingers squeezing the steering column hard enough to leave indents.

Chewbacca howls and points. They can see stars again, set against the black velvet of space. C-3PO becomes even more agitated. "Look, sir, it's—"

"I see it!" Han barks.

Stalactites and stalagmites, like jagged teeth, are closing in on them. Up ahead, the view of space is dwindling, the stars winking out behind stone.

"The cave's collapsing!" cries Leia.

"This is no cave!" Han bellows.

It's true. They are not stalactites and stalagmites. They are teeth.

The cave is not a cave. It is a mouth. The tunnel was not a tunnel. It was a throat. Of something. Something large.

As the massive mouth is just about to shut, the *Falcon*, no bigger than a single tooth, shoots out of the darkness and into the greater darkness of space.

Behind it, a monstrous, wormlike creature—white and eyeless and nearly the size of a Star Destroyer itself—erupts from the hole in the asteroid and tries to swallow the ship up.

The *Falcon* screams ahead and everyone inside screams, too.

But the ship is fast enough—just fast enough—to outpace the space-worm's snapping jaws.

The worm, disappointed, slides back into the asteroid.

The ship, meanwhile, slides into space.

Inside, sweating and heaving, Han guides them toward the edge of the asteroid field.

Where the Star Destroyers are waiting.

LESSON SIGMA:
PUNCHING IN THE DARK

You're going to have someone toss soft objects at you again. You're going to block them away. But this time, your eyes are going to be closed.

Face the person, close your eyes, and breathe. Listen to the room. Feel it.

When you say go, the person is going to—*very gently*—toss these objects at your face and chest. You will try to block them away with your hands.

Listen for the objects. Feel them.

Do not guess. Feel.

You will miss. You will probably miss more than you hit. That's okay. Don't get frustrated. Remember, anger leads to the dark side.

If you can stay calm during this activity, that is more valuable than batting away the objects.

If you can do both, though, you're really on to something.

CHAPTER TWENTY-TWO

T HEY STARE AT the enormous Imperial ships. Everyone's breathing through open mouths. Hearts are beating hard. Everyone except C-3PO, of course, who finds both respiration and circulation superfluous. Still, he's more scared than the rest of them combined.

"Okay," Han says. "Ready for lightspeed."

"Any minute now. . . ." Leia mutters.

Then, out of the blackness of space, a laser blast rocks the *Falcon*. They've been spotted.

"Hold on!" Han bellows. "One . . . Two . . ."

Leia looks in trepidation as another laser bolt screams toward them.

"THREE!"

The four space travelers look expectantly at the stars.

Nothing. Again.

"It's not fair!" Han whines.

The blast rocks the ship, rattling the gears and bolts and cylinders.

C-3PO is frantic. "Sir, the shields are at 40 percent! Another hit like that and we're done for!"

Han looks at his meter readings. "Okay, Chewie. Give me all power to forward shields. I'm going in."

"You're going to attack *them*?" Leia shrieks.

The *Millennium Falcon* dives at the nearest Star Destroyer. Bright green blasts light up the space around them.

"Sir! The odds of surviving a direct attack on an Imperial Star Destroyer are—"

"Shut up!" Leia shouts.

But in case you want to know, the odds of the *Falcon* surviving an attack on an Imperial Star Destroyer are about the same as the odds of a lame, half-blind bunny surviving an attack on a hungry tiger. Give or take.

The ship dives at the Destroyer, lasers blazing.

It is one brave bunny.

On the bridge of the Imperial Star Destroyer, Captain Needa, commander of the vessel, grins. "We have them now."

The *Falcon* hurtles through space, aiming directly, it seems, for the viewing deck of the bridge. Closer, it comes. Closer. Closer.

"Fire!" he cries.

But the red laser blast misses. The *Falcon* is coming too fast, too low.

The captain's face goes white.

The *Falcon* is a hundred meters away. Eighty. Sixty. Forty. Twenty.

"DUCK!" screams the captain. He throws himself to the floor. As if that would do any good.

His face is pressed against the cold, sheer steel, waiting for impact.

Nothing.

When he looks up at last, the sky is empty. Just a million crystalline stars.

"Where are they?" Needa bellows. Behind him, his lieutenants check their readings frantically.

"We can't find them, sir! They've just . . . disappeared!"

"What? Nonsense! Where are they?"

But they search the readings to no avail. The *Falcon* is gone.

An hour later, brave Captain Needa boards a shuttle that takes him from his Star Destroyer to the flagship of the fleet. As he disembarks, his stomach twists into a knot. He listens to his own footsteps echo along the glossy floors of the Imperial ship. He's been a good captain, he tells himself. Everything will be fine.

When he arrives at the bridge, he finds Darth Vader addressing a motley collection of space creatures. There is a T'doshok, a Gand, and a Corellian cyborg, among others. You might not know what any of those look like, but trust me. They're weird. Just imagine some weird dudes, standing around listening to Vader. Oh, yeah, and they're carrying guns. Lots of guns.

They're bounty hunters, by the way. They specialize in tracking hard-to-find pilots, and their ships.

In one corner, standing apart, is a man in a battered, dirty space suit. His name is Boba Fett. He knows the *Falcon* from its days on Tatooine. And he knows the Empire is not the only one who wants it found. That there is money to be made *twice* on this ship. He also knows the man who captains it. And how he thinks.

Darth Vader senses Captain Needa's presence. He stops speaking.

"Lord Vader," the captain says. He can feel his neck beginning to constrict. *Calm yourself,* he thinks.

When the Dark Lord turns, his cape sweeps out behind him, like a stormcloud covering the sun. "What is it, Captain?"

"We—" The captain represses a shudder. "We've lost them."

The grip on his throat is no less painful for being invisible. The air stops flowing to his lungs. Blood ceases circulating in his brain. His eyesight fades to white. . . .

"Apology accepted," Vader murmurs, and turns back to the bounty hunters. Stormtroopers swoop in to dispose of Captain Needa's body.

The *Millennium Falcon* perches on the back of former-Captain Needa's Star Destroyer, just behind its main radar tower—too close to be seen. They say

"Keep your friends close, and your enemies closer." Han Solo is demonstrating the truth of that adage in the extreme.

"Well," Leia admits reluctantly, staring at the bristling gun turret that would be aimed directly at them, if only its operator knew where they were, "that was a neat trick."

"I don't know *what* you're talking about," C-3PO complains. "Captain Solo, you have gone too far!"

"Ararararrragh!"

"No, Chewbacca, I will *not* be quiet! Surrender is a perfectly acceptable alternative in extreme circumstances. The Empire may be gracious enough to—"

Leia reaches over and shuts off C-3PO's audio output speakers. He flails his arms in fury.

Han smiles and leans back in his chair, his hands cradled behind his head.

"Now," the princess continues, "how do we get off?"

"These cruisers like to dump their space junk before jumping into hyperspace. We'll wait for that, and float away with the trash."

"That suits this ship. . . ." Leia mutters.

"Hey!"

"And then? Assuming your garbage camouflage holds up?"

Han leans forward. "Then we've got to find a safe port around here to complete repairs. Any ideas?"

Chewbacca brings up an electronic map on the ship's main control panel. The small crew pores over it. Han groans. "Anoat system. Nothing around here but mining colonies and . . ." He pauses. He is suddenly interested. "And Lando."

"The Lando system?" Leia interjects. "Never heard of it."

"Lando's not a system. He's a man," Han says, warming to the idea. "Lando Calrissian. He's a card player, gambler, scoundrel. You'd like him."

"I don't like scoundrels."

"You like me."

"No, I don't."

Han ignores her. "He's on Bespin. Runs a gas mining colony there. Won it in a card game. We go way back, Lando and me."

"Araaaaaragh."

"That was a long time ago, Chewie."

"What was?"

"Nothing."

"So you can trust him?"

"Trust him? No. But he's got no love for the Empire, I can tell you that much."

Chewbacca lets out a warning bark as he reads the ship's sensors.

They all brace themselves. In a slow avalanche, a mountain of junk—broken machinery, damaged steel, effluent, garbage—floats out into space. The *Falcon* detaches from the surface of the destroyer and floats away with it.

The small crew watches the great warship. They are barely breathing.

The Imperial Star Destroyer fires up its engines,

and then—*boom*—takes off into hyperspace. Han smiles.

Leia lays a hand on his shoulder. "You do have your moments," she says. "Not many, but you have them."

Han prides himself on keeping things pretty cool. But with Leia's hand on his shoulder, and her compliment ringing in his ears, his cool heart beats just a little harder.

Once the star cruiser fleet has completely disappeared, the *Falcon* powers up its engine and leaves the field of space junk, charting a course for Lando's colony on Bespin.

A few minutes later, a small ship—the *Slave I*—nestled among the space junk and filthy with the desert sands of a distant planet called Tatooine, powers up, wends its way through the detritus, and silently follows the *Millennium Falcon*.

— THE —
CITY IN
THE CLOUDS

CHAPTER TWENTY-THREE

BESPIN IS A shimmering pink planet, all gases and clouds like soapsuds. It lies in the fabric of space like a pink marble would lie on a black blanket. Beautiful, out of place.

Floating in the lower atmosphere, crystalline and shimmering like a child's top molded in platinum, is Cloud City, the center of the mining operations on the north side of the planet. A single silver tendril descends toward the gaseous surface of the world below.

The *Millennium Falcon* banks, adjusting its course for the sky-bound town.

"It's a gas mining community," Han explains. "Lando's in charge of the whole thing. Hard to believe, since I've never known him to run anything larger than a card table. But he's been here for years."

Two laser bolts hit either side of the ship, sending it lurching right, then left.

Chewie roars. Han looks at the scopes. Two small patrol ships have taken position just behind them. Through the *Falcon*'s intercom come the words, "You have not been granted permission to land."

Han replies, "I know! I'm looking for Lando! Lando Calrissian!"

"He has identified your vessel," says the voice over the intercom. "You are to follow us. Do not deviate from your course."

The small crew of the *Millennium Falcon* look at one another. "Touchy, aren't they?" C-3PO chirrups.

Leia is looking hard at Han. "I thought you were friends with this guy."

"There's nothing to worry about," Han assures her through gritted teeth.

Leia sighs. "Who's worried?"

The landing pad is empty. Pink clouds float by, pushed by a wind that smells faintly sweet, like someone is cooking pancakes and drenching them with syrup. It's actually the smell of the predominant gas in Bespin's atmosphere, rethen. It isn't toxic to humans. At least, not very.

Han, Leia, C-3PO, and Chewbacca walk down the gangway of the *Millennium Falcon*, the motliest, least impressive crew of a pirate ship this side of the galaxy. They gaze around for some sort of welcoming party.

"Hm!" C-3PO huffs. "No one here to meet us! Quite rude!"

Leia shakes her head. "I don't like this. . . ."

"On the other hand, they *did* let us land," the droid says.

Han tells them all not to worry. But his voice and face are anything but reassuring.

And then, a door on the far side of the platform opens and a dashing man steps through. A long cape dances behind him as he strides forward, and a pencil-thin mustache perches like an ornament just above his lips. A dozen security guards march behind him, followed finally by an officious looking manservant with a bald head and an electronic command system fastened to his ears.

The caped man looks furious.

"See?" Han whispers to his gang. "My friend! Lando!" And then, to Chewbacca, he adds, "Maybe go get the bowcaster."

The man's voice is rising as he approaches. "Why, you *slimy*, double-*crossing*, no-good *swindler*! You've got a lot of *guts* coming here, after the stunt you pulled!" He's coming at Han hard, and with increasing speed. Han sets his feet and curls his hands into fists.

As Lando comes within reach, he throws a hard right at Han. The space pirate ducks—and then is pulled into an embrace.

The landing party stares, confused. But Lando is laughing. "How you doing, you old pirate?"

Lando—as dashing and handsome a man as you've ever met—pulls back and looks at Han. He shakes his head. He's still laughing. "You look like a mess."

"And *you* look like a business- man," Han shoots back.

Lando laughs some more.

The two of them turn and, arms around each other's shoulders, start for the doors. The man- servant with the headset dismisses the guards, who troop in uni- son inside and out of sight.

"Well, he seems friendly," C-3PO announces, falling into line behind the old mates.

"Yeah," Leia mutters. "Charming. . . ."

As they pass through the fine, silvered sliding doors, Lando says, "So, what are you doing here?"

"Repairs." Han gestures back at the *Falcon*. "I thought you could help me out."

Lando looks alarmed. "What have you done to my ship?"

"*Your* ship?" Han stops, and the group following them pulls up short. He is gesturing at his chest with his thumb. "You lost her to me, fair and square!"

"Fair? You never played a hand of cards fair in your life!"

"Are you accusing me of *cheating*?"

"Are you *denying* it?"

The two men glower at each other for a second. Three seconds. Five.

Leia glances at Chewbacca to see if he's got a blaster.

And then the two men break up laughing.

Leia exhales and rolls her eyes. *Men. As egotistical as roosters. And about as smart.*

The corridors of the mining colony are wide and shining. The floors are an expensive, marble-like stone, and frequent windows give out onto a breathtaking view of the lower atmosphere.

"Well," Han asks, "how's the mining business?"

Lando sighs the sigh of the fortunate. "Oh, you know. Never making quite the profit you want. You got your supply problems, then your labor disputes, and once you take care of those, there's—"

Han begins laughing again.

"What's so funny?"

"Listen to you!" Han grins. "Since when were *you* a responsible businessman?"

Lando shakes his head ruefully. "Yeah, I suppose I'm responsible these days. It's the price you pay for being successful."

Leia is watching him. Listening. She notes a sudden something in his voice that she has not heard before. Maybe it's regret, she tells herself.

The group walks on. C-3PO, tottering behind as usual, spies another protocol droid, a 3PO unit, emerging from a side room. "Oh, hello!" he calls.

"E chu ta!" replies the droid.

C-3PO stops, stunned. "How rude!"

("E chu ta," is, of course, Huttese. It is absolutely not appropriate to translate. Maybe when you're older.)

Then, from the room from which the rude 3PO unit just emerged, C-3PO hears the characteristic beeping of an R2. "That sounds just like . . ." C-3PO exclaims. "I wonder . . . !"

As Lando leads the way around a corner and into the next hallway, C-3PO follows the beeping sounds, thinking that maybe, just maybe, he might find his friend.

He does not.

Instead, his eyes get very bright.

And then he is shot, right in the chest.

And he explodes.

LESSON TAU:
PREPARE FOR THE DARKNESS

Scatter objects across the floor. Recruit someone to throw soft objects at you. Stand on one foot. Keep your eyes open. Breathe.

Hop across the floor on one foot, avoiding the scattered stuff. Your assistant should gently throw the objects at you. Bat them away as you hop.

Stay calm. This should be fun.

Difficult things are fun when your mind is not disturbed by fear or anger or pride.

Breathe.

The darkness is coming.

CHAPTER TWENTY-FOUR

LEIA IS PACING in a luxurious apartment. The windows look like paintings too monotonously beautiful to hang in a museum. The furniture is made to look expensive, but was probably mass produced on some moon in the Betthanie system. The carpet makes the place marvelously soundproof. Eerily so.

The doors slide open silently, and Han walks in.

"Repairs are almost finished," he announces. "Two or three more things and we're in great shape."

Leia turns to him. Worry is etched in lines above her nose, and her eyebrows are arched. "The sooner we go the better. Something's wrong here. Where's C-3PO? I haven't seen him for hours, and no one can tell me anything."

Han takes Leia by the shoulders. He gives her his best roguish smile. "Relax. I'll talk to Lando. See what I can figure out."

Leia shakes her head. "I don't trust him."

"Me neither!" Han laughs. "But he is my friend. And besides, we'll be gone soon."

The doors to the apartment open again. Chewbacca enters, carrying a box full of golden parts. An arm sticks forlornly up from the junk. The Wookiee roars.

"What happened?" Leia cries, running to him.

"Aaaaraarragh!"

"What?" Han exclaims. "You found him in a junk room?"

"Aaararararragh!"

"They were going to incinerate him?"

Leia looks desperately at the golden droid's broken pieces. "Can he be fixed?"

"Lando's got the men—"

At exactly the same time, Leia and Chewie say: "No!" and "Araragh!"

"Okay!" Han raises his arms. "Do it yourself, then!"

Chewbacca lowers himself onto a plush footstool, setting the box of droid parts before him. He gazes into it miserably.

Again the doors slide open. This time, it is the suave, smiling Lando Calrissian. He sweeps into the room, his cape swishing behind him like he's some wealthy, complacent superhero.

"Princess!" he exclaims. He approaches her, takes her hand, and kisses it. "You look radiant! You really do belong with us here above the clouds."

Han rolls his eyes.

"Would you care to join me for a little refreshment?" Lando continues, gazing into Leia's face. She returns the stare coolly, and then looks to Han. "Oh, you're all invited!" Lando adds. Han nods. Leia reclaims her hand.

Just then, Lando notices Chewbacca, who is holding C-3PO's head in his great paws. "Having a little trouble with your droid?"

"No," Han replies, brushing past him. "No trouble. Why?"

Lando shrugs and follows Han into the corridor.

As they walk through the glittering halls, Lando talks business. "You see, we've been a small enough operation not to fall under the, ah, jurisdiction of the Empire, you might say."

Leia is ignoring him. She scans each door and corridor for signs of something wrong. All seems normal. Even this worries her.

Han is only half listening to his old friend. "You're not afraid the Empire will find out?"

"Ah, well . . . not anymore." They are approaching the dining room. "You see, we've recently made a deal that'll keep us in business for a good long time."

Han nods. Lando opens the formal dining room's bright white door.

Han and Leia enter—and stop.

Standing at the head of a long, glittering dining table is Darth Vader.

LESSON UPSILON:
THE BEGINNING OF THE END

Now, my young pupil, we are coming to the most difficult tests. The final ones. Succeed in these, and you will not be a Jedi—not yet—but you will know that you *can* be. That you are truly walking the path.

Think of someone or something that infuriates you. Not a pet peeve—like someone peeing on a toilet seat (though that does make me want to take a lightsaber to the entire bathroom). Think of a time when you felt really hurt by something someone did or said. Or think about something that strikes you as so deeply unfair it is almost unbearable.

Let your mind explore those feelings. Your anger. Your rage. Your humiliation.

When I say *go*, I want you to stand and balance a book on your head. Close your eyes. Get someone to throw things at you again. As they do, raise your hands. If you can block the objects, good. If not, that's okay, too.

As you balance that book, and sense the objects, I want

you to spell your name backward. And then the city you live in. And then the state. And then the country. Keep blocking the objects.

And as you do all this, let the anger, the rage that you were feeling, just pass away. Let it lift from you, so you are standing straight and tall and calm. If you are doing it right, you may even start to smile. Despite the objects being thrown at you, and the book on your head, and the angry thoughts that had been exploding through your synapses just moments ago.

Why do you smile? Because it is pleasurable to be at peace. Go.

CHAPTER TWENTY-FIVE

HAN HAS NEVER known such pain.

It rushes through his body in waves—burning his calves, lacerating his thighs, making his stomach churn as if it's being blended, straining his spine and neck until he's certain they will snap, and then filling his head with such a pressure—such a terrible, building pressure—that he decides with what little consciousness he has left that the rest was merely a prelude, and that the real intention of all this has been to make his head explode.

Suddenly, the pain stops. Han gasps for breath. Every cubic millimeter of his body throbs, throbs, throbs.

Now come the questions, he thinks. He waits. He can

hear Vader breathing, somewhere in the room. He must have been screaming, because his ears are ringing and his throat feels as if it's been shredded. *I'll talk,* Han wants to say. *Just ask me and I'll tell you.* He never thought he would be the one to spill the Rebellion's secrets. But he's never felt pain like this.

There are no questions, though. Suddenly, the burning begins in his calves again, making its way up his thighs. "NO!" he screams. "PLEASE!"

Lando is waiting outside the door when Vader leaves the room.

"You said you wouldn't hurt him!"

Vader sweeps by the old cardsharp to where Boba Fett, the bounty hunter, is waiting.

"Once I have Skywalker," Vader intones, his voice a gentle tapping on the galaxy's largest, deepest gong, "you may take him to Jabba the Hutt."

"Hey!" Lando interjects. "That wasn't what we agreed!"

Vader turns, slowly, his cape rustling. "Perhaps,"

he says, "you'd like to renegotiate the agreement?"

Lando's skin is suddenly cold, and his stomach feels like it's being dangled off a bridge. He manages to stammer, "No . . ."

"Good." Vader starts for the door. "Meet me in the carbon-freezing chamber in one half hour." Boba Fett follows him down the corridor.

"This deal gets worse every second," Lando mutters. He follows Vader into the corridor, but then turns left when Vader goes straight. He is hurrying down the shining halls, cursing every gratuitous piece of silver on every gratuitous window. *It's all gratuitous,* Lando thinks. *Pointless. Worthless. What have I done?*

He comes to a door at the end of a hallway and punches a security code into a pad on the wall.

When the door slides open, Lando sees Leia crouched over Han, who looks like a broken doll, while Chewbacca works on reassembling C-3PO.

Han is whimpering. "They didn't even ask me anything. . . ." He seems more than half dead. Leia looks only a little bit better.

When they catch sight of Lando, Han attempts to rise. "Why, you—"

"Save it," Lando snaps. "No time. Look, Vader's agreed to turn Chewie and Leia over to me. They'll have to stay here, but at least they'll be safe."

"And Han?" Leia asks, glaring steadily at Lando.

"Vader's giving him to the bounty hunter."

Han groans. "Then I'm dead."

"He wants us all dead," Leia adds.

But Lando shakes his head. "He doesn't want you at all. He wants someone else. Someone called Skywalker."

Leia closes her eyes, as if, somehow, she has known all along.

"Vader's set a trap for him."

"Of course," Leia moans. "And *we're* the bait."

"This Skywalker is apparently already on his way."

Han staggers to his feet, holding on to Leia and Lando for support. "Well, you fixed us pretty good, pal."

"I'm sor—" Lando is arrested mid thought by a

vicious left hook to the jaw. He falls. Han falls on top of him, still swinging. Lando hits Han in the mouth with an elbow.

"Stop!" C-3PO cries. His head has been reattached to his body. Backward. "Oh, stop that! You won't solve anything that way!"

Chewie drops the droid and helps Leia tug the two men apart. The former friends stare at one another, gasping.

"I've done all I can—" Lando heaves. "I'm sorry. I've got my own problems."

Han wipes blood from his mouth. "Yeah, you're a real hero. Businessman."

The word stings Lando like a swarm of Rattatakian redjackets. He rises and limps from the cell like a whipped dog.

Han lowers himself, gingerly, onto a crate. Leia comes to his side, half smiling. "Well," she says, "I must admit. You certainly have a way with people."

———

The chamber is dark, like a great cave. Somewhere, a massive machine hums. Red lights blink along the walls of the room, while the floor glows a pulsating royal blue. At the chamber's center, there is a pit. Cool carbon gas seeps up from it, seeping into the corners and crevices of hulking industrial equipment.

Darth Vader is inspecting the pit. Boba Fett stands to his left. Lando is hanging back.

"I want Skywalker led in here," Vader intones, his voice somehow even grander and more sinister in the cavernous steel room. "We will freeze him for transport back to the Emperor."

"Lord Vader," Lando says, "we only use this for

carbon freezing. If you put this Skywalker in there, it might kill him."

Vader exhales. He is thinking. At last, he says, "I do not want the Emperor's prize damaged. We will test it . . . on Captain Solo." Vader raises a hand, and four stormtroopers rush out into the corridor to retrieve the space pirate.

Vader's fingers begin to explore the controls of the freezing unit, like a surgeon laying out his knives and scalpels. Carbon gas seeps into the room. Lando shivers.

A moment later, the stormtroopers reappear, flanking Han, Leia, and Chewbacca—with a partially assembled C-3PO strapped to the Wookiee's back.

C-3PO is shouting. "Turn around, you overgrown mop! I can't see a thing! How can I help if I can't see?"

When Han glimpses Lando, he sneers. "Hey, buddy. What's the party for?"

The group of prisoners is led to the edge of the pit.

Lando looks grim. "You're being put into carbon freeze."

"What if he doesn't survive?" Boba Fett suddenly objects. "He's worth a lot to me."

Vader is not interested. "The Empire will compensate you if he dies. Put him in." His fingers are now flying over the controls of the carbon-freezing unit.

"AAAARARARRAAAGH!"

Chewbacca swings his great arms, knocking two stormtroopers senseless. Two more leap onto him, while a third trains his blaster on the Wookiee's chest.

"Oh, stop! Stop!" C-3PO screams.

"Save it, Chewie!" Han shouts. He puts an arm on his huge, hairy first mate. "Listen. I need you to keep your head. You gotta look out for Leia, okay? Don't get killed."

"Ararararaaaaaghhhh?"

"I'll be okay," Han says. He does not sound confident.

"Aaaraararaagh," Chewie howls again. I don't know *what* that means.

Han turns to Leia. Before he knows what's happening, she's kissing him.

Then she whispers, "I love you."

He smiles his crooked smile and winks. "I know."

Suddenly, Han is wrenched backward by stormtroopers. Chewbacca is howling. Leia is choking back tears. C-3PO is explaining the odds of Han's survival. No one is listening to C-3PO.

The stormtroopers thrust the limp, exhausted space pirate onto the platform, which begins to descend slowly. Leia is about to be sick.

She can't take it. She feels like her insides are being torn apart by Alderaanian wolf-cats. She rushes to the edge of the freezing chamber, but a blast of carbon gas shoots up into her face, casting her back. Vader himself is operating the controls.

Chewie roars again. Leia hides her eyes.

"Don't worry!" C-3PO chirps. "He should be quite well protected by the carbonite! If, that is, he survives the freezing process, which I've concluded stands at a 453 to . . ."

More steam. Then a cascade of liquid carbonite, illuminated by a million sparks. They reflect off of Vader's impassive black mask.

The process ends. With a shuddering creak, two great tongs are lowered into the pit.

Up from the gloom they draw a metal rectangle— frozen carbonite. Han Solo's face protrudes from its surface, locked in a scream of agony. Leia looks, and then hides her face again. Chewbacca starts to make a rush for Han, but the muzzle of a blaster reminds him to stay put.

Lando has moved to Han's side, where an electronic readout is registering on a small screen. "He's okay!" Lando announces. "He's . . . hibernating. He's fine."

"He's all yours, bounty hunter," Vader replies.

"Reset the chamber for Skywalker." To the storm-trooper commander he says, "Take the princess and the Wookiee to my ship."

Lando objects. "You said they'd be left with me!"

"I am altering the deal," Vader intones. "Pray I don't alter it any further. Now, leave me. Skywalker has arrived. I can sense it."

LESSON PHI:
FEAR ITSELF

What are you afraid of?

Don't tell me. Don't say it out loud.

I have a policy about that. If you tell someone what you are most afraid of, then one day it might be used against you somehow.

Just think about it. What truly scares you?

Close your eyes. Ask someone to time you, or set a timer, for thirty seconds.

Imagine that terrifying thing. Really imagine it. Picture it before you. Convince yourself that it is happening.

Once the time is up, reset the timer, or have your assistant count again. This time, close your eyes, breathe, and smile.

Fear is in your mind. It cannot hurt you. It has been said that the only thing we have to fear is fear itself. This is true.

You are a part of the Force. What is the worst that can happen to you? You are hurt? You are sick? You pass away?

When those things happen, you are merely changing forms. Becoming something new.

The Force is with you, and you are with the Force.

You and the Force are one.

CHAPTER TWENTY-SIX

YOU STEER YOUR X-wing through the pink, pacific clouds of Bespin.

R2-D2 beeps a question at you.

You can barely hear him. Before your eyes are your best friends. Screaming in pain. Writhing under needles and blades, barking with fear and whimpering in horror.

R2 asks the question again.

"See-Threepio is with them," you respond. "I can sense it."

Your X-wing settles on a deserted landing pad. After scoping it out—to ensure there will be no unpleasant surprises—you help R2 down from his perch at the back of the ship. You consider leaving him behind, for his own safety. But he's a brave little droid, and he could come in handy.

Indeed, you haven't gone three meters when you reach the door to the landing pad and find that it refuses to open. R2 extends his interface arm and inserts it in the universal computer communication port.

You wait. Han and Leia are no longer screaming in your head. Rather, they are silent. Eerily, frighteningly silent. Your palms sweat and your legs quiver. You try to calm yourself. Fear, you know, is your greatest enemy. Fear leads to the dark side. And yet you cannot control the cold sweat beading on the back of your neck.

With a hiss, the door slides open. You sidle into the glassy hallway. The floor shines as your feet side-step their way down its length. Your back remains in contact with the white wall as you move. Your lightsaber dangles at your side. You'll save that for Vader. You unholster your blaster.

Who is here. Suddenly, you sense it. It feels like

someone has walked into a room where you've been sleeping. You sense him, and wake.

His presence is like Ben's once was—except inverted. Every feeling you had for your teacher, your mentor, the closest thing you ever had to a father, is flipped. Love is hatred. Peace is fear. The cold sweat has spread, crawling down your back and up your scalp. Vader, who killed Ben. Vader, who killed your father before that. Here. Waiting for you.

And then, as you look around a corner, you see them. Leia and Chewbacca—with C-3PO tied in pieces to Chewie's back. They are being led by a powerful-looking man with a pencil-thin mustache and a cape, and are surrounded by stormtroopers. Behind the stormtroopers marches a platoon of mining colony security guards. They are all armed.

Chewie must have smelled you. He looks in your direction and howls.

Not a good plan. A hail of laserfire explodes all around you. You duck behind the corner. R2, hiding in your shadow, is beeping and whirring. You lean out and fire a few laser blasts before ducking back behind the wall.

You are breathing hard, but—you are surprised to realize—none of this scares you.

Still, you need to be careful. You don't want to hit the princess.

Leia screams, "LUKE! LUKE!" You pop around the wall again. Aiming a blaster feels different than it used to. You don't have to aim so much. You can feel where the stormtroopers are. As if you were reaching into a box blindfolded, and feeling the difference between socks and knives. You fire at the knives. They begin to fall.

"LUKE," Leia screams again. "IT'S A TRAP! A TRAP!" As soon as the words are out, Leia is picked up and hurried down the hall. "GO BACK! IT'S A—" Doors close, and she, Chewbacca, and C-3PO are gone.

You know it's a trap. You've known since Dagobah. And now that you're here, you know you didn't come to save Leia and Han. If you save them, that will be no more than a side effect. You came here because Vader is here. You realize it now. He called you. To face him.

And you will.

Lando leads the stormtroopers away from their melee with Skywalker, striding far out ahead. He's pressing some buttons on a wristband without slowing his pace.

In another wing of the colony, his bald manservant's headset lights up. The man's eyes fly open. He presses a button by his temple in rapid, silent code.

Suddenly, the stormtroopers aren't following Lando anymore. He feels it.

He turns. He smiles.

The stormtroopers' hands are in the air, and the platoon of security guards are aiming blasters at their heads.

"Take them away," Lando orders the security

guards. The stormtroopers are led to a nearby holding cell.

Lando turns to Leia. "Come on, Princess," he
says. "Let's get to the East Platform. It's not too late
to—"

Lando's words are choked off by two enormous
paws.

"Chewbacca!" C-3PO cries, trying to see from
his position on the Wookiee's back. "What are you
doing?"

The great Chewbacca is choking Lando, that's
what he's doing. He's pushing the gambler down to
his knees, squeezing the air from his windpipe.

"Had—no—choice—" Lando gasps.

Chewbacca squeezes harder.

"Oh, we understand," Leia says, bending over
him. "You had no choice."

"Ha—a—a—"

"Chewbacca, trust him! Trust him!" C-3PO is
crying.

"Ha—a—a—"

Leia suddenly lays her hand on Chewie's arm. "Wait, I think he's saying 'Han.'"

Chewbacca loosens his grip. A little.

Lando gasps with relief. "It's not . . . too late . . . to save Han. Bounty hunter . . . East Platform . . ."

Chewbacca lets him fall. Lando is sucking in air. "That way!" he points.

Chewbacca and Leia stoop to pick up the blasters that the stormtroopers dropped, and then they hurry down the shining corridor. C-3PO calls back, "I'm terribly sorry about all this! He's just a Wookiee, you know!"

Lando drags himself to his feet, grabs a blaster for himself, and follows them, limping and gasping.

They haven't gone far when C-3PO sees a familiar form emerging from a doorway. "Artoo! Artoo!" he calls.

Leia stops, turns, and runs back to the little service droid. Chewbacca follows her. "Oh, turn around!" C-3PO shouts at him. "Please! Oh, you big stupid rug!"

Leia bends down to talk to R2-D2. "Where's Luke?" she demands. R2 beeps madly. Lando has just caught up. He's panting.

"He's gone into the freezing chamber!" C-3PO translates, still flailing and looking in the wrong direction. "Oh, Artoo, how could you have left him alone!"

Lando says, "If we're going to save Han, this Skywalker will have to fend for himself." He looks at the princess.

Leia hesitates. She squeezes her knuckles with her fingers until her hands have gone white. She is choosing between a pile of diamonds and a pile of gold. And she doesn't know which is which. Finally, she says, "If Luke's in there with Vader, we couldn't help him anyway." Her voice is trembling. "Let's go get Han."

The small party, now joined by R2-D2, hurries for the East Platform. The door is sealed, and Lando's mad punching of numbers into a keypad yields no results.

He curses. "They've changed the security codes!"

But R2-D2 has already begun interfacing with the communication port. Within moments, the door slides open. Lando, Leia, and Chewbacca rush through. R2 rolls after them, beeping at C-3PO.

"What do I care about the hyperdrive on the *Millennium Falcon*?" the golden droid snaps at him, bouncing up and down with each of Chewbacca's enormous strides. "We're trying to save Master Han! And what do I always tell you about interfacing with strange computers? You could catch something! Who *knows* who that computer's been interfacing with recently? Did you even *ask*?"

As the group emerges into the pink atmosphere of Bespin, they see Boba Fett disappearing into his small, rusty ship and the hatch swing closed. Lando lets loose a ferocious volley of blaster fire. They all do. No use. They ricochet harmlessly off the spacecraft, like laserballs in one of those laser-pinball machines on Melchior 5.

Lando, Chewbacca, and Leia stand on the

landing pad, furious but impotent, as Boba Fett's ship lifts off the landing pad and swiftly rises into the sweet-smelling clouds, with Han Solo, frozen in carbonite, secure in the cargo hold.

For a moment, they just stare. Then Leia says, "I guess our best bet now is the *Millennium Falcon*."

"Right!" Lando agrees, with renewed hope. "She's the fastest ship in the galaxy!"

Leia, Chewie, and C-3PO all shake their heads.

LESSON CHI:
PREPARE YOURSELF

Get yourself into a comfortable sitting position. It can be in a chair or on the floor.

Get a timer, or ask someone to time you.

You are going to meditate for three minutes. This is the longest I have asked you to meditate. It will not be easy. You will not be able to keep your mind still the whole time. But whenever your mind starts to wander, breathe deeply, and think of that thin, silver thread of breath going in your nose, to the bottom of your belly, and out again. Don't get mad at yourself. Don't be afraid that you will fail. Just relax, and sit, and let your thoughts wander away from you like sheep into a distant field.

When you've meditated for three minutes, open your eyes. Smile.

You have peace. You have compassion. You have patience.

And therefore, you have strength.

Which is good, because you're going to need it.

CHAPTER TWENTY-SEVEN

YOU'VE LOST LEIA and the rest of them, and R2 has lost you. You pad through the white, shimmering corridors. You let your friends slide from your mind. Vader is near. He's the one you must focus on now.

You come to an elevating pad, set back in a recessed alcove. There is a button on the wall. You step onto the pad and push the button. You are being drawn forward. You are not choosing anymore. You are not in control.

The pad is rising now, bringing you into a new room.

A room unlike the sterilized white corridors of the rest of the mining complex. The black walls are barely lit, and where they are it is with winking red lights, while a violet glow suffuses the floor. Cold mist drifts across the cavernous space.

But there is something colder here than the mist.

You hear breathing. Deep. Rhythmic. Metallic.

You look up.

There is a dark flight of stairs. At its head stands a great shadow, with a helmet shimmering in the red and violet industrial dusk, and a black cape swaying gently by the shadow's feet.

It is Vader. As you knew it would be.

His voice is as soft as a lullaby, as sudden as a sword. "You are not a Jedi."

It is not what you expected him to say. You don't know what you expected. But not that. He sounds, almost, disappointed. In you.

He is still speaking. "The Force is with you, young Skywalker. But you are not a Jedi. Not yet."

You resist the urge to respond. To tell him what you've done. And what you intend to do. Instead, you simply ignite your lightsaber. It glows blue in the darkness.

"I have not seen that blade in a long time," Vader says.

You grip it more tightly. "It was my father's."

He says, "I remember." And then he ignites his, an infernal red.

You walk toward one another, you up the stairs, him down.

Your mind drifts to the cave on Dagobah. There, fear defeated you. That will not happen again.

You think of balancing on your hands, with Yoda sitting on your feet. You think of running through the forest, knowing the good wood from the bad, the strong vines from the weak. You think of leading a raging elephoth back to her child.

In those times, you were strong, despite your fatigue, despite the pain, despite your fear.

You take a deep breath and return to that place.

You are but a sword's length away from the

greatest weapon in the galaxy. And yet you will not be afraid.

You sweep your blade forward. Vader repels the blow without effort.

You thrust again. He parries your sword away, steps down the stairs and to the side, and sends a searing swipe at your head. But you knew he would. You saw it, a fraction of a second before it happened. You duck, and Vader's blade cuts an electrical wire, burying you in a cascade of sparks. You slide out of his reach.

"You have learned much, young one."

You lunge at him again, and again. He falls back, parrying both blows—but not quite so effortlessly this time.

"You'll find I'm full of surprises," you say.

Just as you do, Vader swings his blade. You move to the side, above him on the stairs—he is slower than you expected.

And Vader punches your sword-hand with his fist.

Your lightsaber hurtles through the air and clatters to the bottom of the staircase, far out of reach.

You turn back to Vader. Fear has returned to your chest. Behind his mask, you can sense him, almost smiling.

He steps forward.

And then you are flipping backward through the air. You land on your feet, reach out, and can sense that your lightsaber is lying some ten meters away. But what is ten meters? Just the Force, in different form.

Vader charges down the stairs. You call to your lightsaber, and it flies to your hand. It merely needed to trade places with the part of the Force that you were holding, the part that looked like empty air.

Vader is upon you.

You duck and roll and rise to your feet, facing him, sword ignited and ready.

Vader speaks. "Your destiny lies with me, Skywalker. Obi-Wan knew this to be true."

"No!" you shout. A little louder than you intended. Why did you shout?

Suddenly, Vader lunges at you. You step back—and there is no floor beneath you. You are falling. You hit the ground.

He distracted you—confused you. You felt fear, and not the space behind you.

"All too easy," Vader murmurs. He is adjusting knobs on an interface above, and suddenly it is cold. Very, very cold. "Perhaps you are not as strong as the Emperor thought."

Then you are flying upward. Yes. *Flying.* You never knew you could. But you can. You are. Freezing carbon gas is filling the pit, but you are above it now, perched on a pipe attached to the ceiling.

Vader looks down—and then up at you. "Impressive . . ." he says. Is there a smile in his voice?

You drop to a platform opposite Vader and raise your lightsaber.

Vader raises his to meet it.

"Obi-Wan has taught you well. You have controlled your fear. Now, release your anger."

And you feel it. Anger coursing through you. Anger at this man—this Sith—who killed your father. Who killed your master. Who taunts you one moment and praises you the next, as if he were . . .

"Yes," Vader calls to you. "Only your hatred can destroy me."

You swing at him with all your might. He blocks, stepping back. You swing again, and again, knocking him backward. You are trying to control your anger, but you are not succeeding. It is controlling you. Vader is blocking and blocking, but your attack is furious, relentless, blinding. He steps back—and falls.

You stare.

He has disappeared into the gloom. The room has holes in it, it turns out, holes that disappear into a great black mess of pipes. They must lead, you figure, to the central reactor of the mining colony. You switch off your lightsaber, hook it to your belt, and take a long, slow breath.

Then you follow Vader into the darkness.

You are walking through a tunnel. You see nothing, but you can feel the shape of the space—the Force taking the form of a tube, you walking through it. Vader is not here. You press on.

You emerge into a cluttered, dark corridor. Large windows, giving out onto the central reactor core, shed a very dim light. You reach out with your senses. Vader is here, but he is avoiding you. Muddying the Force around you. A pang of fear slaps your heart. He is stronger than you are.

And that's when it hits you. Like a barn being thrown by a sandstorm, right into your body.

You fall, then rise again, throbbing with pain. A giant piece of machinery has clattered to the floor beside you.

You turn to look where it came from—and another crashes into your head. You are on your knees. You raise your lightsaber to protect yourself, but the metal objects are coming too fast. Vader is detaching them from walls, lifting them from the floor, and hurling them at you. You can't see them, you can't sense them—Vader has muddied the Force too much. You are bleeding. You are reeling.

You are losing.

And that's when the biggest one hits you, and you are flying through one of the large windows, glass shattering around you like rain in a storm.

Into the reactor shaft.

There is nothing below you. Nothing for half a kilometer or more.

Time has slowed, which is not necessarily good, because it is merely giving you time to realize that you are falling to your death. Vader has killed you.

And then, as you fall, you realize that there is a gantry platform—a long, thin, steel catwalk—very near you.

You inhale a long, silvery breath.

You reach out.

You are falling, but your hand touches steel. You grab the steel. Your body snaps like a fish at the end of a line.

But your hand is still gripping the steel.

Below you, the reactor core descends into oblivion.

Wind is whipping at your face, you smell your own sweat, and your legs are swinging over the abyss. You kick at the air, but cannot raise yourself to the platform.

Fear is overpowering you now. You look down, and back up. Vader has appeared at the end of the gantry. Towering, enormous, dark. He is walking toward you. His steps echo like the ticking of an enormous clock.

You manage to pull yourself up onto the gantry.

You climb to your feet, which takes no less effort than climbing a mountain.

You ignite your sword. One last stand, you tell yourself. You can beat him.

You try to feel calm.

But you are merely *trying*. So you do not feel calm. Not at all.

Maybe you should listen to Vader. Maybe you should let your anger out. Give in to it.

But you can't even do that. All you feel is fear.

His footsteps on the metal are an enormous clock that is ticking down the seconds to the end of the world. He strides toward you. Dark. Steady. Familiar.

Without warning, you leap at him, your feet leaving the ground entirely, your lightsaber leading like a lance.

He parries.

You land on your feet and instantly thrust.

You smell flesh being burnt. Gas is hissing somewhere.

You stare. Vader stops and looks down.

You have hit him. On the right arm.

You have wounded him.

You feel surprised. Triumphant. You are a great warrior. You have done the impossible.

You have wounded Darth Vader.

You are a Jedi. You have become a Jed—

His sword blazes through the air and cuts your right hand from your arm.

The pain is blinding. But it is instantly eclipsed by your fear. For as you watch the most surreal sight you have ever seen—your own hand tumbling away from you into the reactor core—you see, tumbling with it, your lightsaber.

And now the pain and the fear are one. And they are greater than you. Much greater.

You scramble away from Vader, toward the opposite end of the platform. His voice is calm, knowing. "There is no escape, Luke."

Frantically, you scramble farther away. Suddenly, your legs slip off the thin, crosshatched metal of the gantry. Your stomach hits the platform, knocking the wind from you. You cannot breathe. You are dangling over the abyss again. The wind is rushing by you, pulling you down. You are trying to breathe.

Vader steadily, slowly, advances. "It is useless to resist."

Your one hand is coated with sweat. It is slick, the steel rod is slipping from your grip. Your other arm, sealed with black, burnt flesh, waves out over nothingness. Your breath has returned. It is like little silver-fish, darting away from a shark.

"Don't let yourself be destroyed, as Obi-Wan did." Vader's black helm shimmers in the dim light of the reactor core. His cape sways softly, like silk, with each step he takes. "Do not believe the Jedi lies. There is no life after death. There is only death." Behind his mask, he is smiling. He must be.

You are tired. So tired. Vader is no more than a meter away. You try to inch farther from him, but there is nowhere to go. The reactor core yawns below you.

Suddenly, Vader's voice sounds softer. "Don't make me destroy you, Luke. You don't understand your importance. You have only *begun* to realize your power."

Your hand is slipping. Fear has taken complete possession of you. There is nothing left inside you but fear.

"If only you knew the power of the dark side," Vader says, and looking up at his black mask, his shining eyes, you believe him. He has defeated you. Utterly.

Where is Ben? you think. *Why is no one helping me?*

"Join me," Vader says, "and I will complete your training. With our combined strength, we can end this horrible war. We can bring order to the galaxy."

With one last gasp of strength, you shout, "I'll never join you!" But your voice sounds weak in your ears. Like a petulant child's.

"Join me, Luke Skywalker."

You are trying not to listen to him. *Where is Ben? Why is no one on* your *side?*

"Obi-Wan never told you what became of your father."

Your father. Where is *he*? Rage rises in your chest. "Ben told me enough!" you scream. "He told me you *killed* him!"

And then, there is a sudden silence in the chamber.

And you feel something.

Something you have felt before.

You try not to, but there it is.

You attempt to hide from it. You don't want to know.

But Vader will not let you hide.

"No," says Vader.

He will tell you.

"*I* am your father."

Silence.

"No," you say. And then you scream it. "No! That's not true! It's not . . ."

But you're not arguing with Vader. You are arguing with yourself.

"Search your feelings," he says. "You know it to be true."

Panic is taking over. You cannot see. You cannot feel the Force. You are screaming.

"Luke, you can destroy the Emperor. He has, in fact, foreseen this. It is your destiny. Join me, and together we can rule the galaxy—as father and son."

You fall quiet. You open your eyes. Vader has reached out his hand to you.

"Come with me. It is the only way."

And suddenly, you are calm. As if a great wave had towered over you, and broken, and you were tossed within it. But it has calmed, been pulled out to sea. And you are left, standing on the sand.

You want to be with your father. More than anything in the universe, this is what you want. It is what you've always wanted.

But Vader is not your father. Not anymore.

You let go of the platform and fall into the abyss.

Leia, Lando, R2-D2, and Chewbacca—with C-3PO still fastened to his back—emerge onto the landing platform. The *Millennium Falcon* awaits, framed by the lurid, candy-colored sky. Sweet gases perfume the air.

"She should be ready to go," Lando says, gazing at his old ship.

Suddenly, blaster fire erupts behind them.

"Go!" he shouts. "I'll cover you!" But Leia has already crouched beside him, and together they return the stormtroopers' fire with a ferocious volley of their own.

Chewie sprints for the ship, activates the gangway, and then runs up it, C-3PO still buckled to his big, hairy back.

"Ow!" C-3PO shouts, his head slamming into the doorframe. "Ow again! Bend down, you oversized toupee!"

Chewie bends over, gets inside, and makes his way into the cockpit, with R2 following close behind. Leia and Lando let loose one more fiery round, pinning the stormtroopers back behind the platform doors.

"Come on!" Leia shouts. They disappear up the gangway, and before the stormtroopers can get off another shot, the *Falcon* is sky-bound.

You fall, and fall, and fall. Then you hit the wall of the reactor core. A garbage shoot opens, meant to keep the core clear of detritus. You are sucked in. Barely conscious, you slide through a long chute. Then the chute drops away. You are falling again, and the presence of Vader—of your father, your former father—is fading. You are moving very fast. And now the air is suddenly cold and faintly sweet, and the light is pink and yellow and orange like sunset. Without thinking, you reach out and grab on to a metal rod. It bends—and holds.

You are no longer falling. You wrap your legs around the rod and close your eyes.

Below you, a thousand, thousand meters of gas go floating by. Below that, the boiling surface of Bespin bubbles at a steady six thousand degrees.

You hold on to the metal rod and try not to pass out.

The *Falcon* is speeding into the upper atmosphere. The pink of the sky is fading to navy. Ahead of the ship, there is black, with stars winking welcomingly. And out there, somewhere, is Han.

Your legs are shaking uncontrollably. Your one hand is gripping the cold steel of the metal rod—a weather vane. But your hand is sweaty, and you are

losing your grip. Wind is whipping your face, rocking the flimsy metal vane back and forth. You are framed by the vast expanse of pink Bespin sky. You glance down again.

To fall is to die, for certain.

You try to summon the Force—to accomplish what, you don't even know—but you are spent. Your whole body trembles. There's nothing left. You cannot feel the Force. You can't even feel your feet, as they slide farther and farther down the weather vane.

"Ben!" you scream. "Ben!" It's like calling for your father. The one who acted like your father. Who protected you when you needed protecting, who taught you when you needed guidance. "BEN!"

But he does not answer. You are alone.

And then, as your single hand begins to lose its

grip, you feel something. No. Someone. Another being who is strong with the Force. You feel this person shining through the field of the Force, like a candle in a dark room. And it is close to you.

She is close to you.

"Leia . . . ?" you mutter. How did you never feel it before? "Leia . . ."

And then you hear, *Luke . . .*

LESSON PSI:
A LONG-DISTANCE CALL

The Force is reality. Everything, from electrons to planets, is made up of the Force.

This is why, if you understand it, and have trained yourself, you can sense what you cannot see, you can move what you cannot touch, you can speak with those you cannot hear.

Do that now.

Close your eyes. Meditate for a little while. Then, think of someone who is not nearby. Someone who is in another room, or another country, or maybe not a part of this world anymore. Reach out to him or her with your mind. Let your thoughts trace their way through the Force—around the doorframe, over the ocean, past the gateway of life—to wherever this person is. Put yourself beside this person. Speak to her. Smile at him. Put your hand in hers.

If you are one with the Force, he will hear you.

Really, she is not far away.

CHAPTER TWENTY-EIGHT

———————————— ⚜ ————————————

CHEWBACCA IS STEERING the *Falcon*, Lando is monitoring readouts, and Leia is in the copilot's chair. She is staring straight ahead, but she is not seeing. Nor hearing. She is feeling. Feeling your voice.

Leia . . . you think.

"Luke . . ." she whispers.

Suddenly, Leia spins to Lando. "We have to go back!"

"Back?" he exclaims.

"Araraagh?!" agrees Chewie.

"Luke needs us. I can . . . I can sense it."

"Princess," Lando begins, "Vader is back there, and—"

"Luke needs us!"

"But—"

A deep growl emanates from Chewbacca. Both Leia and Lando look at him. He has already begun to turn the ship around.

"Leia . . ." you call. "Leia . . ."

The pink and orange sky is going black. Not because night is falling. Because you can't see. Your hand is too wet to hold on. Your legs have given up.

And then, there it is, zooming through the atmosphere. The *Falcon*.

You almost let go right then, with relief, with exhaustion.

But you wait.

The ship is under you. The top hatch opens. The dashing man from the mining colony is there, with Chewie. And Leia.

You let go.

On the bridge of the Star Destroyer orbiting the planet of Bespin, Darth Vader watches the monitoring screen. A small, disklike spaceship emerges from the planet's pastel-colored ozone and enters space.

"The *Falcon* is in range, Lord Vader," Admiral Piett announces.

"And you've disabled the hyperdrive?"

"Yes, my lord. As you instructed."

"Good."

"Okay!" Lando shouts, as Bespin fades behind them. "Now let's get out of here!"

He has deposited you on a bed in the medical bay. You are, for the time being, useless.

Chewbacca is flipping switches all over the cockpit. Leia is staring through the windscreen at the lurking Star Destroyer.

"Ready, Chewie?"

Chewbacca roars.

"Okay . . ." Lando says. "Punch it!"

Chewbacca pulls down on the hyperdrive lever and—nothing.

Leia throws up her hands. "This ship!"

"They fixed it!" Lando cries. "They told me they fixed it! It's not my fault!"

On the Imperial Star Destroyer, Vader turns to the admiral. "Prepare your troops to board. Set your weapons to stun."

"Very good, my lord."

Chewbacca and Lando run through the ship, checking valves and adjusting meters.

"What is it? What's gone wrong?" Lando shouts. Chewbacca howls in frustration.

In the medical bay, your eyes are closed, your body limp. The pain in your right arm is a dull, steady throb. You are barely conscious.

And then you hear a voice. Deep and resonant and almost . . . almost pleading.

"Luke."

Your eyes open. Your skin tingles.

"Father," you say.

"Son, come with me."

You are fighting back tears.

"Son . . ."

The word you've always longed to hear. At last. At last.

"Son . . ." Vader whispers. And you can tell—he means it.

In another part of the ship, R2-D2 is welding C-3PO's legs back on to his torso. "Beep beep beep beep boop beep."

C-3PO is not pleased. "Well, I *know* I've looked better! What do you expect?"

"Beep beep beep boop boop beep."

"What do you mean you know why we're not going to hyperspace?"

"Beep boop boop beep." R2 finishes connecting the right leg and starts on the left.

"The computer on Bespin told you? You know

you can't trust strange computers! And who *knows* what kind of diseases you have now! You should be wearing gloves while you're working on me!"

Chewbacca runs by, howling, banging a wrench against random control boards.

Suddenly, R2 leaves C-3PO lying on the floor, partially reassembled, and rolls over to a nearby port. He inserts his communicator.

"What are you doing?" C-3PO cries. "Come back here and put my other leg on this instant! What do you know about fixing hyperdrives? I'm lying here in pieces, and you're having delusions of grandeur!"

In the cockpit, Lando and Leia watch helplessly as they are pulled into the belly of the enormous Star Destroyer. Chewbacca roars and bangs on some more panels.

And then, the stars start to stretch, as if they're being pulled apart from each end. Lando's and Leia's eyes go wide. Chewbacca howls.

Suddenly, they are all flying across the cockpit.

R2-D2 slides wildly back over the floor.

And C-3PO is shouting, "You did it! Oh, Artoo! You did it! You did it!"

In the Star Destroyer, Darth Vader sees the *Millennium Falcon* suddenly disappear into infinity.

He turns away from the monitor.

Admiral Piett loosens his collar and begins, unconsciously, to massage his throat.

But the Dark Lord takes one final glance at empty space and then—he turns away, his head bowed. Not in anger.

In sadness.

LESSON OMEGA:
THE FINAL TEST

Okay, my young pupil. This is it. My last lesson for you.

So far, you have done well. Very well.

But tests are not passed in a moment. Succeeding once is no success at all.

So tomorrow, take a minute before you go to school or work or wherever you go, and meditate. Just for one minute. Breathe.

Then, when you're at school or work or wherever, and you see your classmates or colleagues, think about how they, too, are a part of the Force. They are swarms of particles, nearly identical to you, just separated by a less-densely occupied part of the Force.

And if someone says something you do not like—maybe it is mean, or stupid, or petty—do not say anything in return. Just realize that that person is being influenced by the dark side. And that you don't have to be.

And if, tomorrow, you see someone sitting alone, or

needing defense, or even just needing a smile—help that person out. Even if it makes you look weird or uncool. Remember, Jedi have a higher calling than cool.

Your penultimate test is to live for one full day in harmony with the Force.

Your ultimate test is to live the next day, and the day after, and the day after that in harmony with the Force as well. That is not just *your* ultimate test. It is *the* ultimate test.

There is nothing more to being a Jedi Master.

(Oh, well . . . there are the backflips and lightsabers, I guess. But those will come. Eventually.)

CHAPTER TWENTY-NINE

YOU ARE LYING in a medical bed aboard a rebel star cruiser. You flex the muscles in your right arm. The mechanical fingers, covered with perfectly convincing silicon skin, flex and stretch exactly as you intend. A medical droid pokes your fingers with a needle, and you wince. Then grin.

A voice comes over the comlink next to the bed. It's Lando. "Luke, we're ready for takeoff."

"Good luck, Lando," you reply.

Through the speaker, you hear Chewie yodel.

"You, too, Chewie," you add.

"When we find Jabba and that bounty hunter, we'll contact you."

You agree. "I'll meet you at the rendezvous point on Tatooine."

Then you stand up, stretch, and make your way from the medical center to where Leia is standing by a large window, watching the *Falcon* move away from its dock. She's been listening to your conversation over the comlink.

"We'll find him, Princess," Lando says. "I promise."

You put your arm around Leia and think about how you saw her—no, *felt* her—a shining point of light in the great field of the Force. You look at her.

But she is staring at the *Falcon*. R2-D2 rolls up to the window, followed by C-3PO. You follow their gaze. You think of Lando, and Chewie—but mostly, you think of Han.

You speak into the comlink, but when you say it, you are saying it for them all. Leia and Han, R2 and C-3PO, Lando and Chewie, Ben and Yoda.

Even Vader. You are thinking of him, too.

You inhale, and you exhale. And then you say, "May the Force be with you."

ACKNOWLEDGMENTS

HERE IS A LIST of just a few of the Ben Kenobis and Yodas to whom I owe a debt of gratitude: Sensei Eric Delannoy and Sensei Masahiko Honma. Sarah Burnes and Julie Strauss-Gabel. Dr. Gold and Dr. O. Dan and Alana. Joanne Chan Taylor and Carol Roeder. Pablo Hidalgo and Leland Chee. Elizabeth Schaefer and, especially, the brave and wise Michael Siglain.

Also, Tony DiTerlizzi (you're Ben, because you sent me to Dagobah) and Tom Angleberger (you're Yoda, because your knowledge is so arcane and deep—except when it comes to the Tonnika sisters) and Alex Bracken (who is obviously our group's Leia. Cosign?).

Finally, I want to thank Lauren, who is my Leia, and Zachary, who is my Luke. (What's that, Zach? You thought you were going to be my Han? Please. I'm Han.)

AUTHOR BIOGRAPHY

ADAM GIDWITZ is the *New York Times* best-selling author of the Tale Dark and Grimm series. His books have been named ALA Notables; *New York Times* Editor's Choice; and best book of the year by *Publishers Weekly, School Library Journal*, and *Kirkus*. Adam was a teacher for eight years in Brooklyn, where he currently resides.